CW00860492

Storm Hags

Storm Hags

David Hutchison

Flying Sheep
Publishing

Copyright © David Hutchison. 2023

All rights reserved. No part of this publication may be reproduced, stored
in a retrieval system, or transmitted, in any form or by any means, electronic,
mechanical, photocopying, recording, or otherwise, without first obtaining
the written permission of the copyright owner.

Any references to historical events, real people, or real locales are used
fictiously. Other names, characters, places, and incidents are the product of the
author's imagination, and any resemblance to actual events or locales or persons,
living or dead, is entirely coincidental.

First edition

ISBN 978-1-915579-22-5 (Paperback)

Flying Sheep Publishing.

Seer

Bay of Echoes

Glen of Goats

Stack of The Storm Hags

Mount Suil

Storm Raft

Illustrations Copyright © David Hutchison. 2021

www.davidhutchison.info

Dedicated to my family and friends.

Table of Contents

Seer. © David Hutchison.

The Storm

Kirsty was trying to crawl out of the barrel but the hissing crowd kept pushing her back in with wooden sticks. She made a huge effort, straining, knowing that if she didn't get out soon she would be boiled alive in the hot black liquid. She gave one last final leap and soared up out of the barrel.

There was a crashing noise and Kirsty found herself lying in her sleeping bag on the wooden flooring of the cabin. Her back hurt. The *Marianne* was really tossing back and fore on the stormy sea. Kirsty realised that she had been thrown from the top bunk in the middle of her nightmare. She tried to stand up but the roll of the waves made it extremely difficult. She felt for the side light in the dark. She flicked it on. Her wee brother Angus was still fast asleep in the bottom bunk. His red curly hair stuck out from the top of his tartan nylon sleeping bag. He looked like some kind of Nessie larva. How could he sleep through this?

Kirsty grabbed her mobile from under her pillow. Five a.m. She knew that she would not be able to get back to sleep so she grabbed onto the walls, opened the door and went up the corridor towards the steps to the galley. The door to her parents' cabin was wide open, banging with the pitch and roll of the boat. No one in the bunks. She secured the door. Mother and father must be in the wheelhouse.

Kirsty stepped up into the galley and unclipped the table from the wall. She wedged herself between it and the wooden seat. She reached into the locker and pulled out the keyboard. The screen lit up on the wall. The screensaver of killer whales picking tasty seals off a beach repeated in an orgy of blood. Yeuk! Angus had put it back on when she hadn't been looking.

The boat lurched again and the flat screen crashed off the wall. It scuffed Kirsty on the head. She held her head tightly and tried not to cry as she felt the bump growing through her mousy brown hair. Blast, blast, blast! Kirsty was suddenly sick of everything. Why had her parents decided to quit their jobs, sell up everything, drag her out of school and away from her friends and buy a crappy old boat. It wasn't fair! Blast this head! Blast everything! The screen lay cracked and useless on the table, smeared in red. She took a hand from her head and felt a trickle of blood flow down her forehead and into her right eye. The first aid kit was in the wheelhouse. Kirsty unwedged herself from between the table and seat. She staggered to the ladder and crawled up, knocking on the hatch.

"Mum, Dad!"

There was no answer so she pushed the hatch open.

The wheelhouse was empty. Kirsty crawled out of the hatch and held onto the walls as she looked out the port and starboard windows and then dead ahead. It was still dark outside, the huge swell reflected in the moonlight. The boat was listing. The bow should be pointing into the waves. A broadside hit and they could capsize. Something must be wrong. Her parents would never have left the wheelhouse unattended in such a storm. They must be in the engine room. The bilge pumps had being playing up yesterday. Kirsty grabbed the wheel and steered the boat into the waves as she blinked the blood from her eyes. This was hell. She couldn't leave the wheel to get to the first aid kit. She couldn't look for her parents and her little sprat of a brother was sleeping below, not a care in the world as she, Kirsty MacLeod single-handedly took rein of the *Marianne.*

Oh at first it had sounded exciting when her parents had said, "We're going to buy an old fishing boat and sail around the world!"

What fun! What an adventure! All these exotic places and no more school. She could do her exams online. She had laughed when her friends had started calling her Cutlas Kirsty at school. But on the very first day on the boat she had spewed and spewed until she could spew no more and hurt her throat with dry coughing while the seagulls fought over her stomach contents. That had been a week ago. They had boarded the *Marianne* at Peterhead harbour and spent a day stocking it up with supplies. Then they had got up the coast passing the Moray Firth. They had spent an afternoon in Wick waiting for the tide to turn in the Pentland Firth. Then they had traversed the north coast of Scotland passing Scrabster and the Dounreay Nuclear Power station, sticking out like a football. The swell had calmed down just after Cape Wrath then they entered the Minch; the sea between the Hebrides and the mainland.

"Kirsty, what are you doing?"

Angus's head popped up from the hatch.

"You've got blood down your face."

"I know. Come here and take the wheel!"

Angus clambered up through the hatch and staggered to the wheel.

"Where's Mummy and Daddy?"

"In the engine room. Here. Keep the bows into the waves, like that."

Kirsty let Angus take over the wheel as she got the first aid kit from a cupboard on the wall. She dipped a tea towel in some water from the battered tin kettle wedged on the stove and looked in the mirror on the inside of the cupboard. She winced as she cleaned around the bump as best as she could. The bleeding had stopped and the cut was tiny. Kirsty painted some stinging iodine on it. She covered the cut with one of those blue plasters. The kind that the dinner ladies used at school so that if it fell off into the big pan of mince it would be easier to see. Kirsty thought of the bloody blue plaster mixed up with greasy mince and she rushed for the sliding door of the wheelhouse. She clung to the door handle and boat rail as she emptied her stomach.

A few seconds later she felt much better. The sky was getting lighter and the waves seemed to have calmed down, although still choppy. Kirsty got back into the wheelhouse and strapped on a bright orange lifejacket.

"You okay?"

"Yes, I'm just going to check on Mum and Dad."

Kirsty slid the door open again and held onto the railings. She edged her way around to the stern. The hatch on the engine room was shut. She knocked several times on it. The hatch did not open. She stretched her foot out and got it under the side of the hatch and then pushed it up. The hatch slid over to reveal the engine room below. It was empty. Kirsty could smell the diesel and hear the engine labouring. Where were Mum and Dad?

Kirsty looked out over the choppy grey sea. The sky was brightening up in the east as the sun struggled to rise. She clambered back to the wheelhouse. She noticed that the old cork lifebelt that she had helped to paint a few weeks ago had gone from its rack beside the wheelhouse door. The grappling hook usually wedged behind the stove's chimney had gone too. She looked up at the roof of the wheelhouse. The life raft was still lashed to the roof in its white plastic case. Kirsty slid the door open and entered the wheelhouse. Angus stared at her and looked frightened.

"Where's Mummy and Daddy?"

"I don't know!"

Angus started to sob as he held onto the wheel. Kirsty felt sorry that she had snapped at him and gave him a hug.

"The old lifebelt and the grappling hook have gone. Something must have happened during the storm. Mum or Dad was washed overboard and the other tried to help them."

"Drowned?"

Angus sobbed as he looked ahead. She blinked back her tears as she pulled open a locker.

"We don't know that. Look, the locker is empty! They had their lifejackets on. They could have been picked up by another boat. They're really strong swimmers. "

"You think so?" whispered Angus.

"I'm sure of it!"

"Maybe they swam to that island?" Angus pointed to the starboard window.

"Where?"

Kirsty looked out of the window. Angus was right. In the distance there was an island, blue against the grey sea.

"Angus, head towards that island!"

***

The sea was now calm and it was a sunny morning. Kirsty was trying to read the instructions stenciled onto the side of the radiophone but she could not make head or tail of them. Blast! She should have taken more notice when Dad had showed her how to work it. If the computer had been working she could have sent a message by email to the coastguard but the satellite dish had got broken in the storm. Her mobile had got soaked and died a death. She went into the galley to see if the computer was repairable. She sat on the wooden bench and wiped the dried blood off the cracked screen. She fiddled with the socket in the back of the computer and tried rebooting it. The wee green light came on but the flat monitor screen remained blank.

Kirsty noticed a noise, or more accurately she noticed a lack of noise. The steady vibration throughout the hull of the boat had stopped. Angus' voice called down.

"Kirsty!"

Kirsty sprang up the ladder into the wheelhouse.

"What?"

"The engine's stopped. We're drifting," said Angus.

Kirsty pulled back the sliding door and went to the stern. Blast. What a sailor she was! She had forgotten to batten down the hatch. It had blown off in the wind. The floor of the engine room was swamped in seawater. Kirsty rushed back to the wheelhouse and got a plastic bucket.

"Angus. The water's coming into the engine room. Get something and help me to bail it out!"

Kirsty ran back to the hatch and jumped down into the engine room. The seawater came up to her knees. It was a cramped space, big enough for two adults at a squeeze. Kirsty lowered the bucket and scooped up some water. She passed it to Angus who threw down another bucket. Angus dipped the bucket over the railings into the sea. Kirsty filled up the next bucket and held it up to Angus as he threw the empty bucket down.

They carried on bailing out the engine room until Kirsty's arms were aching.

"Kirsty I think the water's getting higher," panted Angus, looking down at her.

Kirsty looked down. He was right. The water was past her knees now. Kirsty pulled herself up out of the engine room. Angus gave her a hand and helped her to her feet.

"It's the bilge pumps. They won't work when the engine's not running. We must have sprung a plank. The boat is going to sink," said Kirsty.

"Well, we could use the life raft," said Angus.

"Yes. You go down to the galley and bring up all the food you can find. Matches, a pot, bottles of juice. Whatever you can find. I'll get the raft down."

Angus rushed off into the wheelhouse as Kirsty scrambled onto the roof of the wheelhouse. She unlashed the raft and pushed it onto the deck. She twisted a small handle in the direction of a red arrow and the raft popped open. It began to automatically fill up with air. She cut the painter. Kirsty pulled it to the side of the boat and lowered it over the side. She was lashing the painter to the railing when Angus came out of the wheelhouse laden with plastic carrier bags.

"There's water in the galley. Up to my knees," he gasped.

"Get in the life raft and I'll pass the stuff down to you," said Kirsty.

Angus carefully climbed over the rail and got into the raft. Kirsty passed the carrier bags down to him, one at a time.

"I got all the food in the cupboard, matches, candles and the first aid kit," said Angus.

"Right, wait here. I'm going to see if there is any more stuff that we can salvage."

Kirsty ran to the wheelhouse and down the ladder. The galley was flooding with water. She quickly ran through the water to their cabin and gathered up a sleeping bag from the top bunk. The one on the bottom was already soaked in water. Kirsty grabbed some chocolate and cans of Irn Bru from a locker above her bed. She threw them into the sleeping bag along with a couple of wool jumpers and waded back into the galley. She threw an aluminium pot into the sleeping bag, threw the whole lot over her shoulder like a burglar with swag and climbed the ladder. She could feel the boat list as she quickly looked around the wheelhouse. The flares. Where were they? Yes, above the door. She brought the cylinder down and threw it into the sleeping bag. She scanned the wheelhouse again. She grabbed a pocketknife and scrambled out of the door. The deck was difficult to cross as the boat was listing quite steeply.

"Hurry up. We might get sucked down with the boat!" shouted Angus.

"That only happens in films Angus," said Kirsty, although secretly she wasn't sure what would happen. Kirsty quickly passed the bag down to Angus, untied the painter and got down into the raft. Angus pushed the life raft off with an oar and then rowed like mad. The boat listed further over and slipped under the waves. All that was left to show that there had been a boat was an oil slick. Kirsty got out the box of flares and fired all the rocket flares off.

The Bay of Echoes. © David Hutchison.

The Bay of Echoes

Angus rowed closer towards the island. Kirsty looked past him at the island. She could make out several jagged peaks. The hills were partly wooded and swept down to the sea, ending abruptly in a coastline of steep cliffs. Towards the north side dark clouds obscured part of the island. So they headed further south. When they got nearer to the cliffs they saw that they were teaming with nesting seabirds. Kirsty took over the rowing after a while. She rowed to below the towering cliffs but there was no beach to land on. Kirsty rowed parallel to the cliffs, eastwards towards the rising sun while Angus scanned the coastline of grey cliffs splattered in yellow lichen, for a place to land. Kirsty had rowed for over a mile when Angus pointed.

"There. That strange rock jutting out that looks like a dog's head?"

Kirsty turned to look.

"Just past it there's a gap in the cliffs," said Angus.

"I see it."

Kirsty pushed with one oar, pulled with the other and turned the boat. She headed to the narrow gap. It turned out to be the entrance to a concealed bay. They could see part of a pebble beach in the distance. Kirsty rowed through the gap between the high cliffs and Angus guided her past several submerged rocks. The gap opened out into a small bay surrounded on all sides by the high cliffs. Kirsty crossed the small bay to the narrow beach. She pulled in the oars a few metres from the shoreline. Angus got into the water and hauled the life raft out of the sea, over the slippery seaweed up onto the pebble beach. Kirsty got out and helped. They pulled the life raft up past the high tide mark of dried seaweed and onto a thin stretch of grass below the cliff face. Kirsty tied the painter to a pointed rock jutting out of the yellow lichen covered stone of the cliff. Guillemots, gannets, and puffins soared overhead.

They rested against the life raft. Kirsty looked around the sheltered bay. It was about the size of a football pitch. At the far end an impressive waterfall fell over the cliffs. The rays of the summer sun hit it and formed a rainbow.

"We should find shelter. Make a fire. Have some food," said Kirsty.

"I'm too tired. Can't we rest for a bit?" said Angus.

Kirsty also felt tired and the day was still early.

"Okay. Just for a few hours. "

Kirsty emptied the rescued items out of the sleeping bag:

Two jerseys, a lighter, a box of candles, a Swiss army knife, a small pan, 2 tin mugs, a fork, two spoons, bottle of pink grapefruit juice, 2 large bottles of mineral water, 6 cans of Irn Bru, 4 tins of baked beans, 2 packets of onion soup, 3 packets of tomato soup, 8 packets of crisps, a 2 kg bag of potatoes, a packet of rice, a bar of soap and a couple of comic books.

They pulled the raft up at an angle against the cliff face to make a temporary shelter. Kirsty spread the sleeping bag out like a rug. It looked quite cosy. They took off their wet trousers and draped them across the life raft to dry in the sun. Kirsty gave Angus one of the rescued jerseys to use as a pillow. Tired out they both fell asleep in a few minutes.

Kirsty saw the cauldron on the hill in her dreams again. This time however she was not in the barrel. She was a bird flying in a circle above the fire. A man with his hands tied behind his back was being lead up the hill by a crowd of shouting people. He wore dark blue robes and had long brown hair. He stared up at her. He had strange blue eyes; one was paler than the other was. His eyes burnt into her.

...

When Kirsty woke the sun had moved right across the sky and was starting to set. Her trousers had dried so she pulled them on. She woke Angus up. She felt really thirsty and hungry. They each had a can of Irn Bru and a packet of crisps.

"I'm still hungry," said Angus.

Kirsty looked through the food that they had saved and picked up a tin of baked beans.

"Baked beans?"

"Okay, but I'm not eating them cold," said Angus.

"Let's gather wood for a fire," said Kirsty.

They walked along the beach, picking up bleached bits of dried driftwood. As Kirsty was gathering wood she began to have a strange feeling. Her neck tingled and the hair on her neck stood up. She could feel someone watching her. She looked up and scanned the skyline along the cliffs. She thought she saw the dark silhouette of a head with horns against the pink sky but then it disappeared.

"Did you see that?"

"What?" asked Angus.

"Thought I saw something up there. On top of the cliff."

"Mummy, Daddy?" asked Angus hopefully.

"No. It had horns. It doesn't matter. Come on, we've got enough wood now and it's getting too dark to see."

Kirsty shivered even although it was a warm evening. They took their bundles of wood back to the life raft. At a spark safe distance from the life raft, they built a small circle of pebbles. Angus reluctantly crunched up bits of his favourite comic book; "Seordag the Robot Hen". He filled the circle with the paper and Kirsty laid the sticks on top. Kirsty lit the fire and sat back.

They watched the sun as it dipped over the headland to the west and then it was time to put the tin of beans amongst the red embers of the fire. The stars came out. They tried to name as many constellations as they could as they ate their beans from the tin mugs. Kirsty pointed to a bright star.

"Look. That's the Pole Star. Follow it down and there's the plough!"

"Yes. I can see it. Over there is Orion's Belt. It always makes me think of an upside down helter-skelter," said Angus.

A loud wailing filled the air and echoed around the bay.

"What's that?" cried Angus.

"I don't know. Sounds like a wild animal."

"A wolf?" asked Angus.

"They're extinct, in Scotland anyway," said Kirsty.

"Maybe we're not in Scotland?" asked Angus.

"The storm couldn't have blown us that far. We're somewhere in the Minch. Maybe on one of the Summer Isles," said Kirsty.

"Okay. Maybe someone brought wolves here to start them off again. You know like the sea eagles from Norway?" said Angus.

"It's probably just a sheep or a stag. The fire will keep it away whatever it is," said Kirsty.

She got up and added more wood to the fire. She sat back down closer to Angus.

"I'm scared. I want Mummy and Daddy," said Angus as he cuddled up to his big sister.

"Hush. Go to sleep. Tomorrow we'll explore the island and look for them."

The wailing noise sounded once again but this time it came from much further away. Kirsty and Angus pulled the sleeping bag around themselves and stared into the fire. After a short while they were both fast asleep.

The Glen of Goats. © David Hutchison.

The Glen of Goats

Kirsty was lying out on a long steel table. She could not speak as there was something covering her mouth. Doctors with stethoscopes and tweezers were leaning over her, grabbing at her arms, poking her legs.

One doctor with red hair said, "Good muscle development." She nipped Kirsty's arm with pincer like bone fingers.

"Yes, the process works," said a doctor with a warty nose.

"I can't wait for the dressing," said the third doctor. He leaned over, whipped out a long purple tongue with furry edges and started to lick Kirsty's face.

Kirsty tried to scream but she couldn't open her mouth.

She woke up. A fearsome creature blocking out the sky was licking her face. She screamed and the creature jumped away, revealing the morning sky. In front of her was a white goat. It trotted away. Kirsty laughed and wiped her face. The goat stared at her from a distance. She called it.

"Goatie, goatie!"

The goat kept its distance. It occasionally looked up and stared at her as it nibbled at tufts of grass further up the beach. It was a glorious morning and Angus was still sleeping. Kirsty gathered some moss, went to some boulders farther away and did the toilet. She came back, found the soap and went down to the shore to wash her hands in the sea.

"Kirsty!" called Angus.

"It's okay. I'm down here!"

Kirsty came back up to Angus.

"Have you seen the wolf?"

Angus looked puzzled then saw the goat staring at them.

"A goat!" he laughed.

Kirsty showed Angus where to get the moss and the boulders designated as the toilet. They gathered more wood and made another

19

fire. Kirsty got out the saucepan and poured some mineral water into it.

"Onion or tomato?" she asked Angus, holding up the packets.

"Tomato, please," said Angus.

The goat watched them as they drank their soup.

"I wonder how it got down here?" said Kirsty.

"They're really good climbers," said Angus.

"Yes but these cliffs are so steep. There must be another way up them," said Kirsty.

She passed a packet of crisps to Angus. When he opened them the goat came closer.

"Maybe we could catch it and get some milk?" said Angus.

He threw a few crisps onto a rock. The goat cautiously edged forward. Angus kept still. The goat moved closer and bent down and licked up the crisps. Suddenly Angus jumped up and grabbed the goat around its neck. The goat made a whining sound and bolted away. Angus lost his grip. The goat ran down the beach towards the waterfall. Angus got up and gave chase. The goat ran under the waterfall and disappeared. Angus followed. A few seconds later Angus reappeared and ran back up to Kirsty.

"There's a tunnel behind the waterfall. It's big enough to stand up in and it goes uphill," gasped Angus. "It's dark. We'll need torches."

"Okay. Find the candles and lighter. They're in a white plastic bag."

Kirsty rolled up the sleeping bag and put all the food away.

"Found them," said Angus, holding out a candle to Kirsty.

They walked across the narrow grass strip of the bay towards the waterfall. A beaten path lead to a long flat rock next to the waterfall.

"Through here!" said Angus.

Angus stepped up onto the rock. He walked forward a few steps and then disappeared into a dark recess.

Kirsty cupped her hands round her mouth and tried to shout over the noise of the waterfall.

"Where are you?"

Angus appeared again and Kirsty got up onto the flat rock. She took a few cautious steps forward and then followed Angus into the recess. They found themselves on a long ledge behind the waterfall. The water fell like a living curtain.

"Up to the left," said Angus.

Half way along the ledge was the entrance to a cave. They entered the cave and lit their candles. It was a large cavern. The floor sloped upwards towards another cave at the back.

"The goat went up that tunnel," said Angus. He pointed at the dark tunnel.

They walked for what seem like ages, always heading upwards. After a while there was a slight draft and their candles flickered out. As Kirsty tried to light her candle she realized that she could see quite well. They walked a few more paces and around a corner light flooded in. They walked out of the cave into a lush green glen surrounded by rocky heather covered crags. At the top of the glen was a forest of hazel trees. A stream meandered down through the trees to a flat fertile grassy plain. A round stone building stood on top of a cone shaped hill in the middle of the glen. The stream split, encircled the hill then joined up again as it fell over a low cascade. There was a stone footbridge over the right fork of the stream.

On the hills all around were groups of white goats staring down at Kirsty and Angus.

"Let's make for that building on the hill!" said Kirsty.

They walked through the glen on a path that followed the meandering stream. Some of the goats came down from the hills and started to follow them in a line. By the time Kirsty and Angus had got to the stone footbridge all the goats were stretched out in a line behind them.

"Why are they following us?" asked Angus.

"Beats me," shrugged Kirsty.

They went over the bridge and followed the path that wound around the hill in a spiral until at last they were at the top. The stone building looked ancient. It had the shape of a cooling tower, with a low tunnel jutting out as an entrance.

"I think it's a broch. The things Stone Age people made," said Kirsty.

"No. The things that Iron Age people built. We made a model in MacNeil's class last year," said Angus.

A goat nudged Kirsty.

"Hey, get back!" said Kirsty.

"I think they want us to go inside," said Angus.

Kirsty bent her head and entered the tunnel. Angus followed her along the short tunnel. Sandwiched between thick walls of the broch a stone stairway wound up on the left. Kirsty went straight ahead and out into the sunlit centre of the broch. A round space, open to the air. The floor was of short grass apart from a circle of flagstones in the centre. In the middle was a raised stone platform. On it lay a small white skeleton.

"Is it human?" gasped Angus.

Kirsty looked at the shape and size of the skeleton. It could be of a child, but it was all twisted. The bones were very thin and white.

"If it is, it must have been malformed," said Kirsty.

She looked at the head. Its white empty jaws seemed to be laughing. There was a glinting in the sunlight and she noticed a metal pendant previously hidden by the shadow of the skull. She touched it with the end of her candle. It fell down onto the stone plinth. It looked like steel. On it was embossed was a circle within a circle.

One by one the goats outside the broch began to bleat. The bleating grew louder and more manic. It echoed around the glen.

"This place gives me the creeps. Let's get out of here!" said Kirsty.

Angus followed her into the tunnel but when they got to the exit the goats stamped their hooves and tried to head butt them.

"I'm frightened!" cried Angus.

"They won't let us out," said Kirsty.

They moved back into the tunnel and up the stone stairway. Some of the stones were a bit loose in places but they arrived out on the top of the broch without incident. Kirsty looked below. The goats watched them but had stopped bleating by now. Angus sat on the wall.

"We could knock some stones down and kill a few, scare the rest off," he said.

Kirsty shook her head.

"We need to figure out what they want. Is it something to do with that skeleton down below," said Kirsty.

"I don't care what the stupid goats want," said Angus. He kicked at a stone. The stone fell down and just missed a goat. All the goats started bleating again. Angus put his hands up to his ears to block the din. A new sound came from up the glen. A strange electronic pulsing melody. All the goats turned and trotted down the spiral path, over the bridge and then up the glen towards the pulsing marching sound.

"Let's see what they're up to," said Kirsty.

Angus nodded and they went down the stairway and out of the broch. They followed the spiral path down the hill. They crossed the bridge and walked further up the glen. The electronic pulsing melody faded as they saw the line of white goats disappear into a group of hazel trees.

"Come on!" said Kirsty.

They ran along the rough path through the glen. They arrived at the hazel trees and saw that they hid a gully. In the distance they saw the goats following a boy with brown hair. The boy was wearing dark blue robes. Floating in the air in front of the boy was something blue and spinning. It was this spinning thing that gave off the music. The goats followed the boy into a huge cave in the side of the hill and the sound stopped.

"Did you see that thing floating in the air above that boy?" asked Kirsty.

"Some type of toy flying machine. I'd love to get one," said Angus.

"Strange clothes too. Come on!" said Kirsty.

They ran down the path and walked into the cave.

Cut into the bare rock all around the huge cave were stalls. In each stall stood a goat being milked by an automatic milking machine. Set in the wall at the back of the cave was a steel door. The door swished shut.

"Where did he go?" said Kirsty.

"A milking factory. Goat's cheese. I'm hungry," said Angus.

Kirsty went up to the steel door. It had no obvious handle. There was a small design embedded in the steel door.

"A circle within a circle. Like the pendant. It could be a simplified eye shape?" said Kirsty.

"Or a cell with a nucleus?" said Angus.

Kirsty touched it and the steel door slid open revealing a steel compartment.

"A lift. Well here goes," said Kirsty,

They entered the room. The door slid shut and the lift ascended.

The Brotherhood of Gruinsoye

The lift stopped and the door slid open. Kirsty and Angus walked out into a wide stone corridor. A strange machine came towards them. It looked like a green hospital trolley with robotic arms. It moved past, ignoring them. Angus looked at Kirsty.

"Which way?" asked Angus.

Kirsty shrugged and followed the direction of the machine. The corridor opened out into a vast room with row upon row of shelves filled with all sizes of specimen jars. In each of the cylinders strange creatures floated.

"Yeuk. I hate snakes," said Kirsty. She stared at a row of snakes in jars. Large dead cobras, small brightly coloured striped snakes, snakes with two heads, snakes semi hatched out of eggs.

"That's an adder," said Angus. He pointed to a snake about a half metre long with a zigzag mark down its brown back."

They walked along to the next row. The jars were smaller and contained different types of amphibians: bull frogs, tree frogs, cane toads, newts and salamanders.

"Who are you?"

The voice came from an ancient man with long grey hair and a beard. He was wearing a long purple cloak that trailed on the ground. His back was crooked and he held himself up with a gnarled wooden staff. Hanging around his neck was a blue stone, torus shaped like a doughnut. Next to him stood a man, with long wavy black hair, a goatie beard and small sunken eyes. He wore a dark blue robe inlaid with a Celtic pattern of eyes sewn with gold thread. Behind them were two other men wearing dark hooded cloaks.

"A female? In the Monastery? What are you doing here?" said the man with long wavy black hair.

Kirsty moved forward to speak.

"I'm Kirsty and this is my wee brother Angus," said Kirsty.

"Outsiders," said the man with long wavy black hair. The ancient man nodded.

"We were shipwrecked and landed on the beach," said Kirsty.

"We are looking for our parents," said Angus.

"There are others?" said the ancient man.

"We got separated from our parents in the storm," said Kirsty.

The man with sunken eyes said, "I will take some guards to the Bay of Echoes!"

The ancient man nodded and said, "Very well Soyean."

Soyean stared at Kirsty and Angus and said, "A strange catch."

Soyean and the two hooded men rushed off down the corridor.

The old man stared at Kirsty and Angus.

He said, "I am the Keeper."

"You are going to look for our parents?" asked Angus.

"If they are found they will be brought to me," said the Keeper.

"We should phone the coastguard," said Angus.

The Keeper shook his head. "Outside communication is not permitted."

"What do you mean not permitted?" said Kirsty.

He said, "Do not question the authority of the Keeper of Gruinsoye!"

"Gruinsoye?" asked Angus.

The Keeper banged the ground with his staff. "You are on the isle of Gruinsoye. Come with me."

The Keeper walked off down the corridor, not looking back. Kirsty looked at Angus. He shrugged his shoulders. They rushed to catch up with the Keeper. The stone corridor was like a labyrinth. Several times they walked into large halls with several tunnels leading off. They walked past entrances to laboratories where figures in hooded cloaks worked with samples of soil. Other rooms had rows of plants growing in trays of flowing water. Several times Kirsty had asked the Keeper questions but he had ignored her.

Kirsty noticed that the air was getting warmer and wetter as they walked along a tunnel. A few more steps down the tunnel plastic flaps hung from the ceiling created a heat barrier. The Keeper pushed between the plastic flaps. Kirsty and Angus followed him. They found themselves in a massive room with a glass wall stretching across one side. Bright lights glared down from high ceilings. The place was like a hot house, filled with giant tree ferns that reached up to the ceiling far above. They couldn't see out of the glass because it was steamed up. Water dripped everywhere and the air was moist with earthy odours.

The Keeper stopped and said, "A short rest."

He sat down on a worn stone bench. Angus ran up to the glass, wiped it and peered out.

"We're above the Glen of the Goats," said Angus.

Kirsty came up to the window and cleaned the glass with her hand. She looked down and saw the broch on the hill.

"What's this place?" asked Kirsty.

"This is the Hall of the Tree Ferns," said the Keeper.

"I mean the whole place, the tunnels the labs," said Kirsty.

25

"This is the Monastery of the Brotherhood of Sowers," said the Keeper.

Kirsty said, "Brotherhood of the Sowers. What do you do?"

"Yes, what's all this for?" asked Angus.

The Keeper said, "We help the Earth to regenerate. We look after the seed banks."

Angus said, "And how do you do that?"

"If you are destined to join us you will learn our methods,"said the Keeper.

"But why do..?" said Kirsty.

"Enough questions!" said the Keeper.

He walked out of the hot house and down another tunnel. After a few minutes he stopped at a metal door. He touched the symbol and the door slid open to reveal a large refectory cut into the rock. There were seven long rows of tables and benches arranged across a slate floor.

The Keeper said, "This is the Grand Hall."

An end of one of the tables was laid out a buffet of cold meats and seafood.

The Keeper said, "Ah someone has already prepared a meal."

On the wall facing them was an impressive fireplace. The fire burned slowly in the grate. The sticks were hollow cylinders and gave off a peaty scent. On the right hand side of the refectory was a long window seat and a massive stained glass arched window.

He crossed the room to a door on the left and opened it.

"This corridor leads off to several bedrooms and bathrooms. These will be your quarters until your path is determined."

"What path?" asked Angus.

"Yes, what path?" said Kirsty.

The Keeper came back across the room towards the main door and said, "Whether you will join the Sowers or the Mind Casters. Eat and sleep. We will talk tomorrow."

"Mind Casters?" said Kirsty.

The Keeper shook his head and went out of the door. It slid shut. Angus ran up to it and pressed the circle within a circle symbol. The door did not move.

"I think we're prisoners," said Angus.

"Don't be such a drama queen. Probably doesn't want us looking around, you know industrial espionage," said Kirsty.

"Do we look like spies?" Angus shrugged.

Kirsty went over to the huge stained-glass window. It reminded her of the mythical paintings that she had seen in the National Gallery in Edinburgh. The scene was of a fire burning on a hill at the end of a headland. Surrounding the hill was a crowd of people. Amongst them were fairies and imps. A man with long dark hair and a beard was being lead up the hill towards the fire. His hands were tied behind his back. Behind him a barrel was being filled with a dark liquid. The man was looking up to where a torus was floating about three metres above him, giving off shafts of blue light. Kirsty felt a cold shudder going down her back as she remembered her dream.

"I dreamed I was in this scene," she said to Angus.

Angus came across and looked at the stained glass window.

"See that barrel? I'm sure that I dreamt that I was in it on the fire, boiling. Then another time I was a bird flying above it."

"The Brahan Seer," said Angus.

"Who?" said Kirsty.

"The Brahan Seer," said Angus.

"Never heard of him. How do you know that?" said Kirsty.

Angus said, "I was looking at a website about Nostradamus and came across a painting of the Brahan Seer."

"I've heard of Nostradamus. Didn't he foretell the future?" said Kirsty.

"Yes. He was a French Seer. The Brahan Seer; Kenneth MacKenzie, was the Scottish equivalent. He predicted the oil coming to Aberdeen and loads of stuff. He was burned in a barrel of tar by Lady Seaforth," said Angus.

"If the Brahan Seer was so great how come he didn't predict his own horrible death then?" asked Kirsty.

"I don't know. Maybe you can only predict the future for other people," said Angus.

"What's that thing in the sky above him, do you think it's a UFO?" asked Kirsty.

"I think that's the famous Brahan stone; his scrying stone. The equivalent of a crystal ball," said Angus.

"It looks like the flying thing the goatherd was playing," said Kirsty.

"You're right. Look up there above it. See the birds?" said Angus.

Kirsty saw two birds in the sky circling the hill. They were so dark against the gloomy clouds that she hadn't noticed then before.

"Like in my dream. What do the birds mean?" she asked.

Angus shook his head.

"I think there were two ravens and something to do with a curse but I can't remember. It's weird that you had a dream about it," said Angus.

"I'm hungry, let's eat," said Kirsty.

Kirsty went over to the table, sat down on a chair and helped herself to some salmon. She lifted up a jug and poured out a glass of sparkling pink juice. She sipped it. It tasted of cinnamon. Angus came over and sat down. He filled his plate with an assortment of strange looking vegetables. He tried tasting some of them.

27

"Mmmm. This is great. It's like sweet coconut," said Angus. He held up a vegetable that looked like red seaweed.

Kirsty poured him some of the pink juice. Kirsty pulled off her jumper.

"The fire's too warm. I'm burning up," said Kirsty.

"Me too, I'm sweating," said Angus. He also pulled his jersey off.

"What do you think about the Keeper?" said Kirsty.

"The Keeper of Gruinsoye," said Angus. He gulped down more juice. "Sounds like he's part of a cult. You know, like some wacky religious order."

"A cult? And the Mind Casters, whoever they are? It sound like one of those sci-fi films you're always downloading," said Kirsty.

"Phew, it's really hot," said Kirsty as she mopped her brow with a napkin. She got up and started to walk across the room to the fire. She staggered and swayed.

"My head feels funny," said Kirsty. She fell onto the floor.

"Kirsty!" shouted Angus.

He got up and went over to Kirsty. She looked like she was sleeping. He shook her but she would not wake up. Angus's head started to spin and his legs went weak. He sat down then fell into a deep sleep.

The Caldera Gardens

Kirsty saw a boy floating in a tall glass cylinder filled with a greenish bubbling liquid. His wavy seaweed like hair framed a pale face with high cheekbones. Plastic tubes pumped green and white fluids into valves fixed to the boy's stomach. Kirsty moved closer to his face. The eyes opened and he looked back at Kirsty. She jumped back but the boy did not seem to notice her. His eyes were different colours; one dark blue and one pale blue. His eyes closed shut. A blue stone shaped like a torus floated into her mind and there was a blinding flash of energy.

"Kirsty wake up!"

Kirsty woke up. Angus was shaking her. She was lying on a bed in a room with rich red velvet walls. The sun streamed through a tall window. Her head felt sore and her limbs ached as if she was coming down with a nasty cold or flu.

"Where am I?" asked Kirsty.

"One of the bedrooms off the main room. I woke up in the bedroom opposite you," said Angus. "I think they drugged us and then did some sort of experiment on us."

He pointed to a row of little bumps on Kirsty's left arm.

"I have them too," said Angus. He rolled up his jersey. The same pattern of bumps, but one was much bigger and darker than the rest.

"We're being used as human guinea pigs. We have to get away. The door is locked," said Angus.

"What about the windows?" asked Kirsty.

"Come and see for yourself," said Angus. He got up and went over to the window. Kirsty got out of bed and went over to the window and looked out. She nearly fainted as she got vertigo. The window was built into a cliff face. It was a long drop to the rocks and crashing waves far below.

"It's the same as the window in my room," said Angus. "Sheer drop. It's too steep to climb down. Anyway someone's laid out breakfast for us and I don't care if it's drugged, I'm starving," said Angus.

He went off to the main room, followed by Kirsty. They sat down at the table. Under a silver platter was something that looked like a fluffy pink omelette and there was also a rack full of toast. Kirsty ate some of the pink rubbery stuff.

"I think it's salmon mousse. Tastes good anyway," said Kirsty.

The door opened and the Keeper came in.

"How are we feeling?" he asked.

"What have you done to us?" said Kirsty.

"You drugged us and experimented on us!" said Angus.

The Keeper held up his hand.

"You must have been in the broch. You were very lucky. We caught it in time," said the Keeper.

"Caught what?" asked Kirsty.

"A form of anthrax. The Glen of Goats was once used as our testing ground for bio-weapons. Some pockets of it still remain. The broch is particularly unsafe," said the Keeper.

"We saw a skeleton there," said Angus.

"Giles the young goatherd. A brave volunteer who gave his life for the safety of Gruinsoye," said the Keeper.

"My arm is itchy. This spot is sore. Will I be okay?" asked Angus.

The Keeper looked at Angus's arm then smiled.

"You'll live," he said.

"Have you found our parents?" asked Kirsty.

The Keeper shook his head.

"We found your camp at the Bay of Echoes. There is no other place to land on the island except the Dark Shore to the north. I'm sorry," said the Keeper.

"I'd like to go to this Dark Shore to check for myself," said Kirsty.

"That can be arranged but not today," said the Keeper.

"Can we phone the coastguard now?" asked Angus.

"We do not allow communication with the outside world," said the Keeper.

"We must get to the mainland. Can you take us?" asked Kirsty.

"You cannot leave Gruinsoye. You are quarantined. You will be given a series of inoculations over the next few days. If you do not do this you will die," said the Keeper.

"Then when we are cured we can go to the mainland?" said Kirsty.

"I don't think that you understand. You can never leave Gruinsoye. We have to protect ourselves from outsiders," said the Keeper.

"Are we going to be prisoners stuck in this Monastery?" said Kirsty.

"Of course not. You are welcome to go anywhere on the island. I will send you a guide to show you around. You will take the test tomorrow," said the Keeper.

"What test?" asked Kirsty.

"To see if you will join the Mind Casters or the Sowers," said the Keeper.

"But.." started Angus.

The Keeper held up his staff.

"I must go now," said the Keeper.

He left the room, his robes swishing around him. Kirsty looked at Angus.

"Well, do you believe that?" asked Kirsty.

"It sounds feasible enough and there was a skeleton in the broch," said Angus.

"No not that. He's telling us that we are prisoners," said Kirsty.

"We may as well have a look around. We can figure out a way to escape later. Besides we haven't looked all around the island for our parents yet," said Angus.

"They may have made it to this Dark Shore place," said Kirsty.

The door opened and a figure in a green robe and hood came in. He pulled down his hood and stared at Kirsty and Angus. He was slightly older than Kirsty. He had long red hair; green eyes and a short turned up nose sprinkled with freckles. Kirsty was beginning to feel awkward at the way that he kept staring at her.

"It's rude to stare," said Kirsty.

The young man's face reddened.

"I'm Olaf. I'm to be your guide," he stammered.

"I'm Kirsty and this is my brother Angus," said Kirsty.

"If you are well enough I can show you around?" said Olaf.

"I would like to go to the Dark Shore. Our parents might have landed there," said Kirsty.

"It's too late to go today. If you got up early we could go there tomorrow," said Olaf.

"Fine, tomorrow then," said Kirsty.

"What is there to see today?" asked Angus.

"I could show you The Caldera Gardens or perhaps the Eye Tower," said Olaf.

"The Caldera Gardens," said Kirsty.

"The Eye Tower!" said Angus.

"We don't have time to do both properly today," said Olaf.

"Okay, we'll toss a coin for it. Heads I win," said Angus.

Angus tossed a pound coin. "Tails!" he shouted in dismay.

"The Caldera Gardens it is," said Kirsty.

Olaf picked up the coin.

"A lion and a unicorn. The detail is excellent. Is it a talisman?" he said.

"It's a pound coin. You know, money," said Angus.

"Money?" asked Olaf. He turned the coin around. "A woman wearing a crown. Interesting."

"The Queen," said Kirsty.

"You keep it," said Angus.

Olaf grinned and put the coin in a fold in his robe.

"Olaf, who are the Mind Casters?" said Angus.

Olaf said, "It is nothing to fear. If you have a psychic ability, you will become a Mind Caster. If not, you will become a Sower and join the Brotherhood. That is the way it has always been."

"What about me?" asked Kirsty.

"If you have any psychic talent you will join the Mind Casters. If not, the Sisterhood of Sowers," said Olaf.

He turned and pressed his hand on the door. It opened and he went into the corridor.

"Come on!" he said.

Angus and Kirsty followed Olaf into the corridor. The door shut.

"What is that symbol anyway?" asked Kirsty. She pointed to the circle within a circle embossed on the door.

"The torus of truth; a scrying stone," said Olaf.

He turned and walked ahead. Kirsty and Olaf followed him. They walked through tunnels for ages and once Kirsty thought she recognized the laboratories that they had seen before. Several times they had to move out of the way as robot gurneys went past.

"What are they?" asked Angus.

"Robot gardeners. A lot of the work in the nurseries is done automatically," said Olaf.

"How many people are on Gruinsoye?" asked Kirsty.

"Oh about a thousand," said Olaf.

"Were you brought up here?" asked Angus.

"All my life," said Olaf.

"What about your family. Your parents?" asked Angus.

"I have no parents," said Olaf.

"Your mother and father?" said Kirsty.

"I did not need such things. I was created from the seed bank," said Olaf.

"Okay. But you must have had biological parents," said Angus.

"I come from Viking stock. I am from the sixth batch if that is what you mean?" said Olaf.

"Viking stock?" asked Angus.

"Over a thousand years ago a longboat was dragged into the Corriekraken Whirlpool. One Viking survived; Wilfred the Red. He was found wandering the Bog Lands. He integrated well and was added to the seed banks," said Olaf.

"So how many are there on the island from Viking genes?" said Kirsty.

"Twelve of us at the moment. Batch five are all sixty years old. We in batch six are all sixteen years old," said Olaf.

"What about the rest of the island," asked Kirsty.

"Most of the Sowers are grown from the old times stock," said Olaf.

"When was the old times?" asked Angus.

"Many thousands of years ago. When everywhere was covered in ice sheets," said Olaf.

"You must mean the last Ice Age," said Kirsty.

"But that was over twenty thousand years ago," said Angus.

"Time does not matter when you can be renewed from the seed banks," said Olaf.

"So you are saying that most of your people have been grown from seed banks from before the last Ice Age," said Kirsty.

Angus butted in, "I've heard about seeds found in pyramids that grew after four thousand years but I didn't know that the same could be done with people."

"A seed is a seed. The technology is ancient. Your outside world has forgotten many things in the struggle to survive the last time of ice," said Olaf.

"What about the Mind Casters?" asked Kirsty.

"The Mind Casters have been created from the old times stock but over the past few hundred years they have become weaker. Several new specimens have been added," said Olaf.

"New specimens?" asked Kirsty.

"Anyone that the Mind Casters thought might add to the gene pool, enhance their ESP," said Olaf.

"Extra Sensory Perception," said Angus. "I know," said Kirsty.

"Come, we go down this way to the gardens," said Olaf.

They turned off the main steel corridor and down a long tunnel cut into grey rock. Instead of electric light, tarry torches lit the way.

"I'd like to see this seed bank," said Angus.

"It is forbidden to all but the Sowers," said Olaf.

"Why?" asked Kirsty.

"Let us talk of other matters. Here we are nearly there," said Olaf.

The tunnel opened out into a cave. The bright sunlight coming through the cave mouth stung their eyes. It was a beautiful sunny day with a brilliant blue sky, apart from a few dark clouds to the north of the island. The cave mouth was a third of the way up on a sloping mountainside. Below them stone steps zigzagged down to a fertile glen.

"The Caldera Gardens," said Olaf.

The Gardens stretched out into the distance and were bordered on all sides by fantastically eroded mountains.

"The Gardens are sheltered in the crater of an extinct volcano. The rim has eroded over the eons. If you follow the line of mountain peaks you can see how it once was a massive volcano," said Olaf.

33

Every available piece of land was used. Terraces of banked earth overflowing with fantastic plants clung up the sides of the mountains. An orchard of fruit trees extended in a strip below them and along the left side end of the crater.

To the west the Monastery and its nurseries extends to there," said Olaf as he pointed to a circular gap in the peaks making up the northwest rim of the crater.

He gestured to the crater floor. Streams from the slopes were channelled to the fields below. The channels met up and formed a river, which meandered into the distance. In the flat fields grew rows of tall leeks and maize. Many figures, both male and female, in green robes were digging, planting and weeding.

"To the north, beyond the crater rim is the Bog Lands," said Olaf.

"Where is the Dark Shore?" asked Angus.

"Can you see that dark cloud to the right of the Bog Lands?" said Olaf.

"Yes," said Angus.

"That's hiding the Stack of the Storm Hags. They always have a cloud hanging over them. The Dark Shore is near there," said Olaf.

Olaf then pointed to the east side of the crater.

"These vineyards are on the lower slopes of Mount Suil," said Olaf.

"What's that above the vineyards, another entrance?" asked Kirsty.

"That entrance is a tunnel that leads to the Convent of the Sisterhood," said Olaf.

"Oh, so the Sisters and Brothers work together," said Kirsty.

"Yes. The Sisterhood and the Brotherhood are both Sowers, but we live separately. Come let us descend." Olaf started to walk down the steps, cut into the side of the mountain. Kirsty and Angus followed.

"Wow, are they bananas?" asked Angus. He pointed to where towering green plants grew. Blue material was wrapped around a bundle on each plant.

"A hybrid. Tastes like kiwi fruit. The material is to help them ripen," said Olaf.

He turned and carried walking down the steps. Kirsty and Angus followed.

"But how can these grow here. Isn't it too cold? " said Kirsty.

"The Brotherhood has genetically modified them to this climate. They've been spliced with different things. It also helps that we are in the Gulf Stream," stated Olaf, "The Gardens are protected by the mountains and the ground is extremely fertile. We also collect seaweed and guano."

The steps stopped when they reached the orchard of fruit trees. They followed a path through the orchard. Olaf pointed out several trees of interest. He stopped at a tree that looked like an orange tree but had blue fruit. He pulled off one of the fruits and peeled off its citrus-like skin to reveal dark blue flesh.

"Blunge," said Olaf.

Kirsty and Angus each tried a piece of the fruit.

"Tastes like bramble jelly," said Angus.

"Yes, with a bit of liquorice," said Kirsty.

"The Mind Casters boil the skins down for the dye in their blue robes," said Olaf.

He looked around the orchard and then walked up to a tree with red leaves. He picked off a long red pod then prised it open with a knife. Inside were pale yellow flat beans, the size of lemons. He held out the opened pod.

"Here try these," said Olaf.

Kirsty and Angus tried them.

"Custard and mint sauce," said Angus. He spat his out.

"I quite like it," said Kirsty.

Kirsty went up to a tree laden with golden apples. She pulled one off and took a bite.

"This is the most delicious apple I've ever tasted," said Kirsty.

"I helped to create that variety. They are are Avalon apples," said Olaf, with a certain amount of pride in his voice.

They heard a musical sound in the distance.

"That's the same music as in the Glen of the Goats," said Angus.

The path opened out to a clearing, at the centre of which was an ornate white marble building. It was pentagon shaped. Moorish fretwork windows were set into each side.

"The Mendelian Temple," said Olaf.

A boy with brown hair was sitting cross-legged on the front steps of the building. He seemed familiar to Kirsty but she didn't know why. Floating in the air in front of him was a small blue torus spinning slowly around. The boy concentrated and the torus spun round faster as the electronic pulses speeded up.

"What is that?" asked Kirsty.

The boy looked up, the torus fell to the stone step and the music stopped. He looked at Kirsty and stared. She smiled back.

Olaf said, "Kallid. This is Kirsty and Angus."

Kallid nodded to Kirsty and Angus.

"Do you look after the white goats?" said Angus.

"Yes. How do you know?" asked Kallid.

"That's where I saw you!" said Kirsty.

Olaf said, "Kallid. Explain the function of the scrying stone."

Kallid said, "I am a student of the Mind Casters. I have some limited precognition ability. Sometimes I can see into the future. I've a bit of telekinetic power too," said Kallid.

"What's telekinetic power?" asked Kirsty.

"Being able to move things with your mind," said Olaf. "Carry on, Kallid."

"This scrying stone tones up my mind and enhances my ability. I also have fun making music with it," said Kallid

Kallid concentrated on the scrying stone as it floated up into the air. It spun round slowly and started to give off a pulsing hum. Kallid seemed to go into a trance for a few seconds. The torus slowly floated down to the ground.

"It's unclear but I sense danger," said Kallid.

"Don't worry. Kallid's better known for his musical talents than his soothsaying," said Olaf.

Kallid grinned shyly.

"I'd like to try it. Have a shot of boosting my mind," said Angus.

Kallid said," Concentrate on the hollow centre of the stone. Imagine your thoughts are pouring through that space."

Angus frowned and concentrated on the stone. Nothing happened. Angus sat down, crossed his legs and concentrated on the stone again.

Kallid said, "Image that your thoughts are like solid matter. They have weight and they can exert force."

Angus tried to focus his entire mind on the stone but still nothing happened.

Angus said, "I don't get anything. Kirsty you try."

Kallid looked at Olaf.

Olaf said, "Let her try."

Kirsty sat down and stared at the stone. To her surprise it instantly moved along the marble temple step.

Kallid said," Focus on the centre of the hollow space, not the whole stone."

The stone rushed up into the air, above the roof of the folly then it came falling to earth.

"Woah gently does it," shouted Kallid.

Kallid concentrated his mind. The stone slowed down and stopped in the air at his eye level.

"That was astonishing," said Olaf.

"No one has shown so much latent energy before. I must go to the Temple of Suil at once. The Mind Casters must be informed," said Kallid.

"You can inform Lady Morgana that I will bring the outsiders to the Temple of Suil tomorrow evening. For now I am going to show them the rest of the gardens," said Olaf.

Angus said, "Who's Lady Morgana?"

Kallid said, "She's the leader of the Mind Casters and new blood like me. She's cloned from the great Seeress Mother Shipton."

Angus said, "Mother Shipton. We went to see her cave. The petrifying well was cool."

Kallid got up, bowed and walked along the path that branched off to the east.

"I've never even been able to even bend a spoon before," said Kirsty as she shrugged her shoulders. "So what happens at the Temple of Suil?"

Olaf said, "The Temple of Suil is where the Mind Casters hold their most important rituals. "

"I know that the Sowers take care of the gardens. So what do the Mind Casters do?" said Angus.

"With their enhanced mental power they have shielded us from the outside world for centuries," said Olaf.

Angus said, "What do you mean?"

Olaf said, "They cloak Gruinsoye in a screen of invisibility. Ships pass by without seeing us. We don't show up on your technology called radar either."

Kirsty said, "How did we find the island then?"

Olaf said, "Perhaps it was your latent telepathic ability or even the electric charge built up by the storm. The Mind Casters will no doubt make it their priority to find out.

Angus said, "Where is this Temple of Suil?"

Olaf said. "On the summit of Mount Suil. Come let me show you."

Kirsty and Angus followed Olaf out of the temple and along the path. They soon came out of the orchard. Neat square patches of fields stretched away into the distance. Olaf pointed to the slope on the right side of the crater.

"These are the foothills of Mount Suil. Look up there. See that curved peak. Like an eagle's beak on its side?" said Olaf. He pointed to a rocky summit that towered above the surrounding mountains.

"Yes," said both Kirsty and Angus at the same time.

"The temple is on a plateau on the top of that peak. Can you see it?" said Olaf.

"I think I can see something but it's so far away. It looks like a really difficult climb. How are we going to manage to get up there tomorrow?" asked Kirsty.

"Yes, I'm no mountain goat," said Angus.

"It's much easier than it looks. There is a path on the north side," said Olaf.

They walked past a marshy plot where huge plants grew. They had stalks as thick as an arm that ended three metres high in a large fluffy white ball.

"They look like bog cotton," said Kirsty.

"Correct. A genetically modified version and one of our most useful plants. The white heads are used in cloth making. The stalks are crushed and the oil is extracted for use in lighting. The rest is used as fuel for heating."

They walked to the next field where giant maize was growing. Kirsty caught a glimpse of a massive dragonfly flying amongst the plants. It landed on a leaf. The dragonfly was as big as a dinner plate. It had beautiful shimmering wings. She pointed it out to Angus.

Kirsty gasped, "Look at that huge dragonfly!"

"We breed them too. They eat pests," said Olaf. He sat down on a low wall.

Another giant dragonfly flew past, wings glinting in the sun as it chased a cloud of midges. Olaf stood up.

"Come we still have plenty to see," said Olaf.

Kirsty was getting up when she heard screaming and a loud clicking noise. From round the corner a young man in green robes came running towards them. His hood had fallen from his face and he looked so much like Olaf that he could have been his twin.

The young man shouted, "A grak, a grak!"

The man ran past them. A smell of rotten fish wafted through the air. Around the corner slithered a weird beast that made a low clicking noise. It looked like a monkfish and it was the size of a very large dog. It propelled itself forward on the ground like a snake; its bumpy brown skin glistening in the sunlight. When it saw the group of people it stopped. It gave out a deep clicking noise like a motorbike revving up, showing a mouth full of cruel sharp teeth.

"What is that?" said Angus.

"Back to the folly!" shouted Olaf.

They ran back along the path to the small white building. The grak made its strange call again and slithered after them. Angus fell on the first step of the folly.

"I've twisted my ankle," he shouted.

Olaf and Kirsty helped him up. Angus leaned on their shoulders and hobbled as fast as he could up the steps. They got inside and Olaf managed to push the doors shut. The grak was furious and rammed the doors again and again. It clicked and revved in rage. Kirsty peered at it through the fretwork window as it circled the folly. It caught her eye and reared up its underbelly against the window. Kirsty jumped back from the window. The stench of rotting fish was unbearable so Kirsty held her jumper up to her nose. Olaf looked at her.

"It's okay. It can't get in here. It'll soon get bored and move off," said Olaf.

"What is it?" asked Angus.

"A young female grak. An unfortunate genetic experiment using amphibians. They usually keep to the Bog Lands in the north, beyond the crater rim," said Olaf.

"So why's it here?" asked Angus.

"It's mating season. When they're in heat they lose their senses and occasionally swim up through the underground river," said Olaf.

The grak rammed at the doors again.

"It looks really dangerous," said Kirsty. She still had her jumper held to her nose.

"It'd rip us all to shreds if it could get in here but only because it's in heat. At all other times the grak are sluggish and you can hardly smell them at all," said Olaf. He went over to a window and looked through the patterned holes. The deep clicking call of the grak was fading into the distance.

"I think it's gone away but we better wait a while to make sure," said Olaf. He took off his green cloak and laid it out on the folly's floor.

"We may as well sit down and be comfortable," said Olaf. He gestured for Kirsty and Angus to sit on the robe. Kirsty and Angus sat down.

"I'm tired. It's probably the inoculations and all this excitement. I'm going to have a wee nap," said Angus. He yawned and curled up on the floor. Soon he was snoring. Kirsty looked down at her brother. She took off her jumper, rolled it up into a pillow and tucked it under Angus's head.

"How can he go to sleep at a time like this?" she said.

"You're very close aren't you?" said Olaf. He stared at Kirsty. "What's it like to have a family?"

"Angus. Sometimes it's not easy. We used to fight like cat and dog but since the shipwreck he's been great," said Kirsty. She stroked a hair that had fallen over Angus's face. Kirsty thought about her parents and blinked the tears back.

"A family. My parents. You only appreciate them when they've gone," said Kirsty.

"I'm sorry if I upset you," said Olaf. He blushed.

"It's okay. The guy that ran past us. Isn't he your brother or something? He looked like your twin," said Kirsty.

"Kind of. That was Aleron. We're more than twins. We're clones, There are five of us," said Olaf.

"Clones?" said Kirsty.

"All the Brotherhood and Sisterhood are clones. There are several different castes. I'm from Viking genes. Kallid is from Brahan genes. Most of the others go way back to the old times," said Olaf.

"I've heard of Dolly the Sheep, but I didn't think that we could make human clones yet," said Kirsty.

"The Brotherhood has been using cloning techniques for thousands of years. Have you heard of the Saliens?" said Olaf.

"I think so. Is that some UFO cult?" asked Kirsty.

"They believe that we were seeded here on this planet by aliens," said Olaf.

"I remember now. They claimed that they had cloned humans but wouldn't give any proof," said Kirsty.

"One of the Brotherhood betrayed us. He passed on our cloning techniques to them," said Olaf.

"What happened to him?" asked Kirsty.

"The Mind Casters took care of him," said Olaf.

Angus made a snorting noise and woke up. He sat up and looked around.

"Where am I. Oh! Has the grak gone yet?" said Angus. "The awful smell has gone."

Olaf stood up and looked through the fretted windows on all sides of the folly.

"All clear. Let's go," said Olaf. He flung the doors open.

"I think we've had enough of the gardens today. Come let's go back," said Olaf.

Kirsty picked up her jumper and pulled it on. Angus got up and tested his ankle. He winced and grabbed Kirsty's arm.

"Okay?" asked Kirsty.

"Not too bad if I lean on you," said Angus.

Angus held onto Kirsty's arm as they cautiously stepped out of the folly and down the steps. There was no sign of the grak. Olaf started to walk along the path back through the orchard. Angus and Kirsty followed him. It was starting to get dark. Rustling sounds echoed through the orchard. Kirsty thought she caught glimpses of something moving in the shadows.

"I think there's something following us," said Kirsty. She stopped. Angus took his hand from her arm.

"The grak?" asked Angus.

"We would have smelled it," said Olaf.

"I probably imagined it. I'm a bit jumpy," said Kirsty.

"It is not good to be out at dark. There may be other things worse than graks that hunt at night," said Olaf.

"What like?" asked Angus.

"I don't know. A Sister disappeared last month. Several Mind Casters novices went missing before that. Always at night," said Olaf.

"Let's get a move on then!" said Angus.

He leaned on Kirsty's arm.

They quickened their pace through the orchard. Soon they had reached the steps cut into the mountainside. Above them the rocky face was bathed in a gorgeous pink, the reflection of the sunset. They climbed up the zigzagging steps to the cave mouth. When they got to the entrance they sat down for a rest. Kirsty looked across the valley as the sun set over the mountains. In the distance she heard the faint sound of a grak. She shivered and stood up.

"Don't worry. It's an echo from the bog lands," said Olaf.

They walked back up the tunnel and through the maze of corridors. Eventually they arrived back at the Grand Hall. The fire had been lit and the room was welcoming.

"I'll see you both in the morning, goodnight," said Olaf.

"Night," said Kirsty.

"See you tomorrow," said Angus.

Kirsty went to her bedroom. A bath of hot water scented with herbs had been made ready. Grey robes, in her size, had been laid out on her bed. She ran through to Angus's bedroom. Angus had the same in his bedroom.

"I'll see you in a while. I'm having a bath," said Kirsty.

"Ok I will too," said Angus.

They both had their baths, changed into their grey robes and met up in the main room.

The long soak in the bath had healed Angus's ankle.

While they had been steeping in their luxurious baths someone had come in and laid out a supper on the table. There was a dish that tasted like nut roast, a bowl of vegetables that looked like red broccoli and a tray of leeks stuffed with goat's cheese.

Kirsty was just finishing off another piece of the nut roast when Angus stood up from his chair.

"I've only just noticed it!" exclaimed Angus.

"Just noticed what?" asked Kirsty.

"Look. Look at the window, the man, the Seer. Who does he look like?" said Angus.

Kirsty looked at the Seer in the painting and then she suddenly noticed what Angus had seen.

"Kallid. It looks like a bit like Kallid, or what he would look like grown up," said Kirsty.

"Yes, that's what I thought," said Angus.

"Olaf told me that he was a clone so Kallid probably is too. When was the Seer alive?" said Kirsty.

"In the sixteenth or seventeenth century. That is if he really did exist and is not just a legend," said Angus.

"The boy in my dream," said Kirsty.

"What?" said Angus.

"There is some kind of experiment going on. I've been dreaming about it. It's something to do with making a clone of the Seer, for some reason," said Kirsty.

"Ask Olaf in the morning. I'm tired. I'm off to bed," said Angus. He yawned and said, "Night Kirsty."

"Night Angus," said Kirsty. She sat and watched the burning embers in the fire. She recognized them as the dry stalks of the gigantic bog cotton she had seen earlier. What a long but exciting and terrifying day she had had. Kirsty got up and went to her bedroom. She opened the window slightly and heard the surge of waves crashing against the rocks below. She pulled the window full open and stared out at the glittering sea. The moon was almost full and the velvet sky was studded with stars. Kirsty went over to the bed and undressed. She stretched out on the comfy bed. What would Lady Morgana and the other Mind Casters have in store for her tomorrow? A thousand other questions tumbled through her mind as she gradually fell asleep.

Stack of the Storm Hags. © David Hutchison.

The Storm Hags

Kirsty had the dream of the boy in the glass jar again. He was staring at her from behind the glass. His mind was calling for her to help him. Kirsty had the feeling that there was something important that she had forgotten. If she remembered this thing she would be able to help the boy.

Kirsty woke up to the sound of seabirds outside the window. Daylight streamed through the lead glass windows. Kirsty stretched and got up. She went over to the window and opened it. She looked out onto a lovely clear sunny morning. The sea stretched away for miles into the flat horizon. She got cleaned up in the bathroom and then went to meet Angus in the Grand Hall.

"Morning, Try the boiled eggs," said Angus. He dipped a piece of toast into a huge egg.

Kirsty and Angus had just finished their breakfast when the door opened and Olaf came in.

"I thought that this morning we could go to the Dark Shore," he said.

"Yes. To see if there is any sign of our parents," said Angus.

"Yes. They could have landed there," said Kirsty.

"The Dark Shore is on the western slope of Mount Suil. We will go to the Mind Casters on the way back."

Kirsty and Angus followed Olaf into the corridor. They went back through the Hall of Tree Ferns and then the tunnel with the plastic flaps. A few tunnel forks later and Kirsty had lost all sense of direction. Olaf turned to look at her.

"We will be out of the tunnels soon," said Olaf.

A few minutes later the tunnel opened out to a cave mouth. Kirsty recognized the crater far below. They were on the eastern rim of the Caldera Gardens. To their right the rim fell away into the sea. Ahead a jagged peak arose from the rim.

"Mount Suil," said Olaf.

"Why is it higher than the other mountains on the crater rim?" asked Kirsty.

"It wouldn't have been at one time. There is a layer of quartz on the summit of Mount Suil that stopped it eroding as fast as the rest of the rock of the crater rim," said Olaf.

"Topped with quartz. Like that mountain we climbed in Assynt last summer," said Angus.

"I remember," said Kirsty.

After about ten minutes Olaf pointed out a path leading off the main path.

"That path going down there. That's the cliff path to the Convent of the Sisterhood," said Olaf. "Most of the Sisters use the easier way; a tunnel cutting into the Gardens."

"Can we take a look?" asked Kirsty.

"Maybe you can sometime. Men are not allowed. Come we've a long way to go!" said Olaf.

For the next hour they walked along the rocky path as it curved around the eastern side of the mountain. Olaf pointed out various native plants. His knowledge of plants was extensive. Everything seemed to be used for some purpose: red berries that grew on a flat stunted bush could be used to remove poison from snakebites, yellow lichen that was used in a potion to help one sleep, purple flowers that helped with headaches.

The sun was high in the sky when they came to a fork in the path.

"The left path curves up and towards the Temple of Suil. The right path goes down to the Dark Shore. Come let's go to the Dark Shore," said Olaf. He took the right path.

After a short while the path descended into a gully. In places the gulley had been widened. The path steepened and eventually became steps cut into the side of a cliff. A metal chain was fixed into the cliff at waist height. It was fastened every few metres.

"In case it's windy," said Olaf. "I'll go first. It's easier if you keep as close to the cliff face as possible."

Angus followed Olaf down the steps. Kirsty held onto the chain and looked over the side. Her heart leapt into her mouth as she saw the drop to the rocks below.

"Come on Kirsty. Just don't look down," said Angus.

Kirsty held onto the chain with both hands and went down the steps sideways like a crab. It took longer, but this way she didn't get vertigo. After what seemed like a lifetime Olaf declared that they were nearly there.

"I see it. I see it!" shouted Angus.

Kirsty chanced a glance down. She was roughly four metres above the beach. Olaf and Angus ran down the last few steps and waited for Kirsty at the bottom.

Finally Kirsty stood on the Dark Shore. The sand was almost black. She bent down and cupped some sand in her hands. Amongst the sand grains were larger pebbles full of holes and very light.

"Why's it black?" asked Kirsty.

"It's volcanic sand," said Olaf.

Angus threw a black pebble into the sea. It floated.

"Wow!" said Angus.

Kirsty looked across the beach.

"I can't see any sign of our parents. Are you sure that is the only other place to land?" said Kirsty.

"The beach stretches for several miles along this north coast. See that high rock in the distance sticking out of the sea at the far end of the beach? " said Olaf.

Kirsty and Angus both nodded.

"That's the Stack of the Storm Hags," said Olaf.

Kirsty and Angus could make out that the stack had something built on top of it but it was too far away to make out properly.

"Past the stack there is another beach of sorts. More like mud flats. No one could land there though because of the Corriekraken," said Olaf.

"Corriekraken. What's that, a sea monster?" asked Angus.

"It's a strong whirlpool just offshore. Anything approaching from the sea would be sucked into it," said Olaf.

"What do the Storm Hags do?" asked Kirsty.

"They spend most of their time squabbling amongst each other but they do have great powers when they get round to working together," said Olaf.

"Can we visit them?" asked Angus.

"Only if they ask for you. They are very secretive," said Olaf.

"Oh," said Angus.

Angus picked up a pile of pebbles and wandered down to the edge of the sea. He started to throw them out to sea. Olaf and Kirsty walked along the beach. One stretch of sand was bluer than the usual black and it made a funny squeaking noise as they walked over it.

"What's that?" said Kirsty.

The dark blue sand rippled under her feet and she fell over. The blue ripple continued along the beach for about five metres then it formed a crude face in the sand. It gave out a hearty laugh.

"What's doing that? Is there some creature in the sand?" asked Kirsty.

"Patches of the beach are sentient. The dark blue bits. Left over from one of the Mind Caster experiments. They are quite harmless and fun. Try it," said Olaf.

"Try what?" said Angus as he came running up to them.

"Try thinking of a shark for example," said Olaf.

46

Kirsty looked at the sand and imagined a small shark. The blue sand shimmered and a shark fin made of blue sand quivered up out of the beach. It swam along the beach.

"What's that!" gasped Angus.

Kirsty stared at the shark fin and it rushed towards Angus. Angus was about to scream when the fin suddenly dissolved into a flat patch of dark blue sand.

"You try Angus!" said Kirsty. "Look at a blue patch of sand and imagine something."

Angus shrugged his shoulders then stared at a blue patch of sand. A large hairy blue spider quivered as it crawled up out of the sand. It slowly moved towards Kirsty.

"Don't. You know I hate spiders!" said Kirsty.

Angus laughed as the spider started to chase Kirsty down the beach. She ran past another blue patch and out of it sprouted a baby elephant. The baby elephant squashed the spider. Olaf laughed when he saw Angus's disappointed face.

The afternoon passed quickly as the three of them created living sand sculptures. They had competitions to see whose was best. Angus created a pirate ship and Kirsty made a huge whale that sunk the ship. Olaf thought up a harpoon and launched it at the whale. Angus turned the harpoon into a bunch of toy cars, which raced in all directions across the beach. They kept a lookout for any signs of their parents but they found nothing.

They ambled along the beach towards the cliffs and the Stack of the Storm Hags.

The stack thrust upwards from the base of the slippery promontory. On the very top brooded a dark cloud. Through swirling gaps they could occasionally glimpse a rickety shack of driftwood, perched like a badly stuffed bird ready to topple and fall into the sea at any moment.

"How do they get up and down?" asked Kirsty.

"Up there. See that rusty lump of metal jutting out? "said Olaf.

Kirsty and Angus nodded.

A small metal crane stuck out over the edge of the stack with a rope hanging from it. Tied to the end of the rope was an orange fisherman's basket

"That dark cloud is weird. It's like it's stuck to the top. Blue sky everywhere else," said Kirsty.

"Storm Hags always have a pet cloud close by," said Olaf.

"What are they like?" asked Angus.

"Nellbridy's tall and skinny with white hair. Strict but fair. Kerigayle is fat with flaming red hair, and a temper to match. Halibutina is short and bent over like a hook. She's the easiest to get on with.

47

"What do they wear?" said Kirsty.

"Dresses and hats made from seaweed," said Olaf.

"So, how come they're so powerful?" asked Angus.

"They've got the original scrying stone," said Olaf.

"The Brahan stone?" asked Angus.

"Yes, that's the one. It belonged to the Brahan Seer. Boosts their natural power. They can command storms, cause blizzards, earthquakes and tsunamis,"

"What about the stone that Kallid had?" asked Kirsty.

"Mind Caster stones are weak. They have only been touched by the Brahan stone."

"How did the Storm Hags get their hands on it?" asked Angus.

"Their pet ravens Birog and Crok. The Seer threw his stone out to sea when he was being dragged up the hill to his death," said Olaf.

"Boiled in a barrel of tar!" Angus chipped in enthusiastically.

"Horrible," said Kirsty.

"As I was saying, he threw his stone out to sea. The ravens caught it between their beaks and carried it back to the Storm Hags," said Olaf.

"But the Seer was meant to have been killed hundreds of years ago. Are the Storm Hags that ancient?" asked Angus.

Olaf continued, "The Brahan stone slows down the aging process but..."

"Look! There's someone at the winch," interrupted Kirsty.

Up on top of the stack the mechanical arm swung round and the plastic basket was being lowered. The basket swayed in the sea breeze as it descended to the rocky promontory.

As it landed on the rocks a pair of ravens swooped down and screeched. They flew several times around Kirsty and Angus then landed on Olaf's shoulders. Olaf took some bread out from a fold in his cloak and gave each raven a piece.

"Good girl Birog. Good boy Crok," said Olaf.

The ravens made appreciative croaking noises.

"You are to go up," said Olaf. He pointed to the basket. "It'll just about hold the pair of you."

Angus checked the rope. It was made of frayed strands of plastic and didn't look very strong. Kirsty looked into the fisherman's basket. It was covered in barnacles and seemed safe enough, although a bit smelly.

"Why not!" said Kirsty.

She climbed into the basket. Angus squashed in beside her.

"I'll come back for you later," said Olaf.

He waved and walked back along the beach. Crok flew off to follow Olaf. Birog flew around Kirsty and Angus then settled on the basket edge. The basket lurched into the air. It swung back and fore as it climbed up into the sky.

48

Kirsty was trying not to look down at the sea and the rocks below. Angus looked at the face of the stack as they rose. Curious puffins looked out of nests at them as they moved upwards.

As they got nearer to the top windows appeared, made from tiny circular pieces of different coloured glass and difficult to see through.

"Beach glass built up like stained-glass windows," said Angus.

It started to spit rain.

Birog flew off the basket and up into the mist.

Soon Kirsty and Angus were level with the top of the stack. Some of the mist cleared and they got their first proper look at a Storm Hag.

Kirsty had expected a little shrunken old witch. Halibutina did have a curved back but she was still well over six feet tall. She had a strong weather beaten face; dark skin blue with scabby white bits peeling off.

Her hat, made from different coloured strands of seaweed, poured round her hunched shoulders like dreadlocks.

Birog was perched on her shoulder. Halibutina pulled a lever and the basket swung over the cliff and onto the flat rock floor.

"Hails o' sleet. Com oot. Com oot!" Halibutina screeched as she tied the rope.

Kirsty and Angus climbed out and stepped onto a flat rocky area. Plastic and wooden fish boxes were piled up all around, some filled with nets, others spilled over with odd pieces of flotsam. Through the mist they made out the driftwood shack. It had portholes and an upturned old boat for its roof. A tin chimney, like the funnel of a ship, jutted out from its tarred planks and black smoke belched out, mixing with the mist to create a smog.

Halibutina waddled across to the shack and pulled back a tarpaulin to reveal a doorway. She gestured for them to enter.

"You go first," said Angus to Kirsty.

Birog flew through the opening. Kirsty entered. . The large room stunk of kippers. Off to one side was a staircase winding down to a lower level. In the centre of the room was a stove. Its doors were open and a peat fire burned merrily away. An ample woman with red hair looked up from poking the fire. Her skin was blue black. She smiled, revealing green teeth. She wore an outfit made from long thick strips of the kind of seaweed that looks like a crocodile's back.

"Ah. Ootliners. Halibutina gae an pou tha' tarpaulin shut," she said.

Halibutina pulled the tarpaulin back across the door. She gently nudged Angus and Kirsty forward.

"Ma sister Kerigayle," said Halibutina.

"I'm Kirsty and this is my brother Angus," said Kirsty.

Kerigayle bent down and stuck her tongue out at Angus. It was green and furry. She grabbed Angus's arm in pincer like bony fingers.

49

"Muckle o' meat on this ane," she cackled.

Angus jumped back in horror. Kerigayle laughed.

"Dinnae greet. A 'm jestin'. Here ye're shivering, " she said. She pulled a fish box from a corner and sat it on its side in front of the fire. She patted the fish box.

"Come sit'n'wairm yersels up," she said.

Kirsty and Angus sat down next to the fire.

"We're looking for our parents. We were shipwrecked in the storm. Have you seen them?" asked Angus.

Kerigayle and Halibutina looked at each other guiltily and shook their heads.

Kerigayle said, "Sorry about the storm."

On top of the stove there was a large pan boiling away. Halibutina went over to it and gave it a stir with a wooden spoon.

"Yese be hungered?" asked Halibutina, "lempet broth."

She sipped some of the soup and frowned, "Kerigayle hae a taste o' it."

Kerigayle went over to the pot and took a sip of the soup.

"Needs som'it wi' a bit o' kick," she said.

She bent down and picked a red jellyfish out of a bucket and threw it into the pan. The sisters seemed to have forgotten that Kirsty and Angus were there. A scuffling noise came from below. Nellbridy, the third sister, came up the winding rock staircase. She was very tall and wrinkled with blue black skin and seaweed dreadlocks. She wore a long dress made from shimmering mackerel scales.

"Halibutina, Kerigayle. Whaur's yer mainers? Ye didnae tell me we hae veesitors!" she said as she reached the top of the stairs.

"A seen thaim on the shore. Ane o' thaim hae the pouer," said Halbutina.

"Aye the stane it glow'd," said Kerigayle. She pointed to the ceiling. Angus and Kirsty looked up. The roof had loads of things hanging from it. There were dried and smoked fish tied on ropes. Bundles of netting and old glass buoys. A metal hook hung down lower than everything else. Caught in this hook was a glittering blue torus. It was double the size of Kallid's scrying stone. Nellbridy crossed the room and lifted the stone off the hook. It brightened slightly as she grasped it. Nellbridy came over to Angus and Kirsty.

She held the stone above Angus's head as if he was a king about to be crowned. Nothing happened. She gently placed the stone on top of Angus's head. Still nothing.

"Mus'be the quean," said Halibutina.

Nellbridy held the stone over Kirsty's head. It started to get brighter and began to pulse. Nellbridy placed the stone on Kirsty's head. It felt cool but not cold.

Images rushed through Kirsty's head. A man being dragged up a hill and towards a fire. Ravens circling overhead. The scrying stone pulsing with light and sound. The boy from her dream pleading for help. A chorus of voices asking questions. Kirsty was spinning around in a whirlpool and she was scared that she would be sucked down and drowned.

Nellbridy pulled the stone from Kirsty's head. The images vanished and Kirsty was back in the room. Nellbridy placed the stone back on the hook. The three Storm Hags looked at each other and muttered.

"Unco strang," said Nellbridy.

"Byordinar'," said Kerigayle.

"Aye she mus' hae oor bluid in her veins," said Halibutina.

"Whaur ye fae quean? Wha's yer kin?"" asked Nellbridy.

"Where am I from?" asked Kirsty.

"Aye," said Nellbridy.

"Edinburgh. My brother and me are MacLeods," said Kirsty.

"Tha' cannae be richt," said Kerigayle.

"It is. We're trying to find our parents," said Angus.

"A can tell ye this. Ye'r nae brither 'n' sister. That's certaint," said Kerigayle.

"But Kirsty's my sister. My daddy's Alistair and my mummy's Janet," said Angus.

"He's telling the truth," said Kirsty.

"Naw," said Kerigayle. Halibutina and Nellbridy both shook their heads.

"The quean hae Storm Hag bluid in her veins. Thar's nae mistak," said Halibutina.

"Whiten veesions did the stane gie ye?" asked Kerigayle.

"Oh the same as my dreams. A man being dragged up a hill towards a fire. A boy asking me for help," said Kirsty.

"We think it's something to do with the Brahan Seer," said Angus.

"Yes there's stained glass window at the Monastery that's like bits of my dream," said Kirsty.

"A ken the windae," said Nellbridy.

"A've seen the loun in ma dreams an'a. Daes he hae ane daurk blue ee. The tither muckle whitely?" asked Kerigayle.

"He looks blind or something in one eye," said Kirsty.

"Tis the Seer nae dou't. He's sending us a wairning," said Nellbridy. The sisters nodded.

"A warning of what?" asked Kirsty.

"A dinnae ken yet," said Nellbridy.

"Mebbe tae dae wi the murthers," said Halibutina.

"Olaf said people had disappeared," said Kirsty.

"In the Caldera Gardens," said Angus.

"A thocht it wis graks," said Kerigayle.

"Graks ma lempet!" said Halibutina. She stood up and the air darkened above her. A crack of lightning flashed through the portholes and there was a peal of thunder,

"Thare she's awa," said Nellbridy.

"Ance a stairt a cannae stap," said Halibutina. The thunder and lightning repeated.

"Yese better gang awa. I'm stairting an aw," said Kerigayle.

A gust of wind built up around her. Kerigayle's seaweed dress and hair twisted and turned.

"We bodden the Brotherhood nae mair storms for the neist week," said Nellbridy as she lead Kirsty and Angus to the doorway. Thunder rumbled and lightning crackled across the sky. Rain poured down on the stack.

"Bide here and haud the tarpaulin open!" said Nellbridy. She ran out into the rain and came back with a bucket of water. She put it down in front of Halibutina and Kerigayle. Nellbridy picked some sponges from a string hanging from the roof. She threw one to each of her sisters. Halibutina and Kerigayle sponged down their seaweed clothes. The thunder and lightning calmed down. The rain stopped. Birog came out from some hideyhole in the roof and perched on Halibutina's shoulder.

"Mak haste. A'll tak yeses back doun eenou!" said Nellbridy. She walked out of the door towards the winch. It was still misty outside. Kirsty and Angus made their way to the basket and climbed in.

"We'll see yeses again. Fareweel," said Nellbridy.

"Bye," said Kirsty and Angus.

Nellbridy hoisted the bucket up and over the side. She started to let the rope out. Kirsty and Angus held on tightly as they descended through the mist.

Half way down the mist cleared and they could see the beach stretching out to the cliffs. Olaf was in the distance. Crok flew up and circled around Angus and Kirsty then flew up into the mist above.

Soon they had landed safely on the rocky outcrop. They got out of the basket and went down the beach to meet Olaf.

"How did it go?" asked Olaf.

"We went down a storm," laughed Angus.

They walked back across the Dark Shore. The sentient blue patches of sand had disappeared.

"Where's the blue sand patches?" asked Kirsty.

"The lightning frightened them off. You won't see any more of them today," said Olaf.

They walked across the beach. Angus occasionally ran down to the water's edge and threw stones in. Eventually they arrived at the bottom of the steps cut into the cliff. Kirsty found it much easier going up than she had going down. Everyone was out of breath when they reached the top of the cliff.

"I'm tired. I need a rest," said Angus. He sat down on a large flat rock. Kirsty and Olaf sat down next to him. They looked across the beach towards the Stack of the Storm Hags. Dark clouds still covered the top half of the stack. Olaf produced a bottle from a fold in his cloak and passed it to Angus.

"Pomegranate juice," said Olaf.

Angus took a long drink. He passed Kirsty the bottle and she took a long swig of the pink juice.

"You know, I could really be a Storm Hag," said Kirsty.

"What's that?" asked Olaf.

"The Storm Hags thought that Kirsty had their blood in her veins," laughed Angus.

"Do you not remember what our Mother told us? About how our Granny was a silkie?" said Kirsty.

"Oh yes! I forgot about that. Wasn't she the only survivor of some shipwreck?" said Angus.

"Yes. The only survivor. Granddad found her washed up on the beach," said Kirsty. "That's where the silkie bit comes in. Finding her on the beach," said Angus.

"They never discovered the name of the ship although they tried to look up the shipping logs," said Kirsty.

"He took her home and married her," said Angus.

"I don't suppose a silkie is related to a Storm Hag. Is it, Olaf?" said Kirsty.

"I'm not sure. What's a silkie?" asked Olaf.

"One of the Seal people. They are said to lure sailors to rocks and drown them," said Angus.

"Like the sirens?" said Olaf.

"Yes but they weren't any use at singing. They would sometimes come ashore. When they removed their big sealskin coats they passed for human," said Angus.

"It's just an old myth," said Kirsty.

"But the Storm Hags are real so maybe Granny was a silkie," said Angus.

"Olaf. Do you have any food hidden away in your cloak? I'm quite hungry," said Kirsty.

"We never did get to taste that limpet broth," said Angus.

"Kirsty grimaced, "I didn't like the look of it."

"The berries on that bush over there are quite safe to eat," said Olaf.

He got up and went over to a low bush laden with purple berries. He picked several and brought them back to Kirsty.

"Fool's Milk berries," Olaf said.

She tried one. It tasted slightly of cheddar cheese.

"Mmm. Not bad," said Kirsty. She got up and went over to the bush. She picked quite a few of the wee purple berries. She brought a handful back and shared them with Angus.

"We'd better head off now. We've got to be at the temple before sunset," said Olaf.

They all stood up and started to walk along the path. They came to the fork in the path and headed towards Mount Suil.

Mount Suil. © David Hutchison.

The Mind Casters

Kirsty and Angus followed Olaf up the side of the mountain. After about ten minutes the path went up into a narrow gulley. At the entrance to the gulley was an animal horn hanging from a rock by a silver chain. Olaf picked up the horn and blew on it. The warbled sound echoed through the gulley and down the mountainside.

"To announce our arrival," said Olaf.

They walked up the narrow gulley, which opened out into a wider area, flanked on either side by strange buildings. They had thick round stone walls each about a metre high. On top of these walls were structures like wigwams. Some of these wigwam roofs had sections open to the sky and large telescopes poked out from them.

"This is Suil, the village of the Mind Casters," said Olaf.

Men and women started coming out of these buildings. They all wore the usual Mind Caster garb of dark blue robes with scrying stones hanging from their necks.

Olaf went up to the entrance of one of the largest buildings. Soyean came out of the building holding the hand of an old woman. She was short and wore the usual dark blue robes of the Mind Casters. Her hair was hidden beneath a high purple headdress. She moved with a solemn dignity that belied her bright mischievous green eyes.

Olaf bowed and said." Greetings Lady Morgana."

Lady Morgana nodded her head.

I have brought the outsiders for the test."

"Very well. Let us make our way to the temple. Soyean lead the way!" said Lady Morgana.

Soyean smiled at Kirsty and Angus. It wasn't a nice smile. It was a cunning smile. Soyean clapped his hands and a procession of Mind Casters gathered around Lady Morgana. Soyean lead the way up a steep path zigzagging up out of the gulley. Olaf gestured Kirsty and Angus to follow. The steep path opened out onto a plateau on the top of Mount Suil.

"The Temple of Suil," said Olaf.

The temple was a circle of massive standing stones, which glinted in the sunlight. It was as if the mountain had a halo. In the centre of the circle was a stone platform.

"Cool. It's bigger than Callenish," said Angus.

"Remain here, outside the circle," said Olaf.

The group of Mind Casters split up and spread out around the stone circle. Each Mind Caster stood with their back against one of the tall stones, facing the centre. Lady Morgana sprinkled some liquid from a vial over the stone platform. She turned and looked at Olaf.

"Bring the boy first," she said.

Olaf nodded and said, "Angus come with me. Kirsty, you wait here!"

Angus followed Olaf into the middle of the circle.

"Lie down on the platform," said Olaf.

Angus did as he was told. Olaf rearranged Angus's arms and legs so that his feet were facing the sun.

"Whatever happens don't move until I tell you!" said Olaf.

Angus nodded. Olaf came back to stand beside Kirsty. Lady Morgana moved to the remaining empty space in front of one of the stones. She held out her scrying stone and began a low chant. Kirsty could not make out the words. It sounded more like a humming noise. The other Mind Casters joined in. The scrying stones began to glow. The chanting got louder and all of the scrying stones got brighter. All at once shafts of blue light emitted from the centres of all of the scrying stones. They beamed onto the platform under Angus. Angus began to glow. The pace of the chanting speeded up. Slowly Angus started to levitate. When he was about a third of a metre above the platform the Mind Casters slowed down their chant. Angus slowly sunk back down onto the platform and the glow around him faded. The beams of light from the scrying stones cut off. The chanting got quieter and quieter until only Soyean and Lady Morgana were chanting. They too stopped chanting.

Soyean shouted, "We have a new Sower."

Olaf went into the circle and shook Angus.

"What happened?" asked Angus.

"You are now a Sower," said Olaf.

Angus got to his feet. He shook a bit as he walked back to Kirsty.

"What was it like?" asked Kirsty.

"I don't remember anything except feeling cold," said Angus. He shivered.

Lady Morgana took out the vial again and sprinkled more liquid over the platform.

"And now the girl," said Lady Morgana.

"Come," said Olaf.

Kirsty followed him into the circle. She stretched herself out on the platform in the same way that Angus had.

"Keep still and don't worry about it," said Olaf.

He walked out of the circle and stood beside Angus. Lady Morgana started up the chant again. Soyean and the other Mind Casters joined in. Rays of blue light beamed from the scrying stones and swathed the platform. Kirsty began to glow. The chant got faster and Kirsty began to levitate. She rose higher and higher, until she was a metre above the platform, enveloped in a glowing sphere of intense aquamarine. A wind started up. The sky darkened as storm clouds gathered overhead. Angus heard a rumble of thunder. There was a flash of lightning. One of the Mind Casters shrieked and fell to the ground. There was another flash of lightning and two other Mind Casters screamed then fell down. The sphere of green light around Kirsty exploded and everyone was thrown to the ground. Kirsty was flung several metres from the platform. She lay stretched out on the grass. Angus struggled to his feet and ran to her.

"Kirsty, are you alright?" shouted Angus, over the noise of the wind and thunder.

Kirsty didn't move. Angus shook her. She felt as cold as ice and her lips had gone blue.

"Kirsty. Wake up!" he shouted.

She did not wake up. Olaf came over and felt Kirsty's wrist.

"She's unconscious," shouted Olaf.

Soyean helped Lady Morgana to get up. They came over to Kirsty.

"The power she has!" shouted Soyean.

"Help me carry her," shouted Olaf.

The other Mind Casters had got to their feet. Lady Morgana gestured for two of them to help with Kirsty. Their cloaks flapped in the wind and the lightning sparked across the dark sky as they carried her out of the circle. Angus held onto Kirsty's hand but had to let go when they went down the steep path to the village. They took Kirsty into the largest of the Mind Caster houses; Lady Morgana's. They laid her out on a fur rug in front of a roaring fire. Kirsty made a groaning noise and awakened. Angus held her hand.

"Where am I? What happened?" asked Kirsty.

Kirsty sat up. Lady Morgana handed her a glass.

"Drink this. It will make you feel better," said Lady Morgana.

Kirsty drank deeply from the glass.

"I remember a green light and then.." said Kirsty. She dropped the glass and fell asleep.

Lady Morgana looked at Angus and said, "She's very weak. We need to get her back to the Monastery. The Keeper will be able to treat her."

Soyean said," I think she should stay here."

Olaf shook his head. "It's not just from the test. She and Angus both need to get their booster injections for the anthrax. "

"Very well. I will arrange for a stretcher," said Soyean. He left the room and came back a few minutes later with a stretcher and four Mind

Casters. They placed Kirsty onto the stretcher. Lady Morgana tucked a rug around her. The Mind Casters lifted Kirsty up and out of the house.

Lady Morgana said, "The girl will brought back here in a few days. Tell the Keeper to expect me at the Monastery tomorrow. There is little time to waste. I will teach her some mind expanding exercises."

Angus and Olaf followed as the Mind Casters carried Kirsty down the side of the mountain. The storm had died down but the sun had set. Clouds obscured the moon and stars so Olaf led the way with a blazing torch.

Angus was exhausted by the time they got back to the Monastery. Kirsty was put to her bed. The Keeper arrived and gave her an injection while she slept. He also gave Angus an injection. Angus had to look the other way as the needle went in. He didn't mind injections as long as he couldn't see it going into his arm.

"Your sister will be fine in the morning," said the Keeper. He got up and left.

Olaf came into Angus's bedroom.

"It seems as if your sister will become a powerful Mind Caster. When she has recovered she will move to the village on Mount Suil. She will be taught by Lady Morgana," said Olaf.

"What about me?" asked Angus.

"Oh you will stay here at the Monastery and learn the secrets of the Sowers," said Olaf.

"But I want to stay with Kirsty!" said Angus.

"You cannot change what will be," said Olaf. He blew the candle out beside Angus's bed, left the bedroom and closed the door.

Angus was very tired and fell asleep.

The Seed Banks

Angus was woken early by Olaf. He was carrying a dark green bundle, which twinkled with silver.

"Morning," said Olaf.

"Hi. How is Kirsty?" said Angus.

"I've just looked in. She's fine but still sleeping," said Olaf.

"Good," said Angus.

"Are you getting up? There's breakfast set out for you in the Grand Hall," said Olaf

"Yes Olaf. What's that you've got?" asked Angus.

"Your new cloak. Fit for an apprentice of the Sowers. See!" said Olaf. He held out the robes. Angus got out of bed and took the cloak from Olaf.

"Thanks, I'll be through in a minute," said Angus. He went to the bathroom and got washed. He came back through to the bedroom and tried the coat on in the mirror. The dark green cloth had been decorated with silver thread. On the back there were two tori entwined. On panels going down the front embroidered leaves twisted amongst strange fruits. He went through to the Grand Hall. Olaf was standing beside the Seer stained-glass window. Angus sat down to a breakfast consisting of different types of bread with blunge jam and a golden Avalon apple.

"What's planned for today?" asked Angus as he wiped some jam from his mouth.

"I'm going to show you where the different nurseries are. Later the Keeper will show you the seed bank," said Olaf.

"How about Kirsty. Is she coming?" asked Angus.

"No. She has now joined the Mind Casters. They're forbidden to enter the seed bank. You both need some final injections over the next few days or she would have been sent to the Village of Suil by now," said Olaf.

"Why are Mind Casters forbidden to enter this seed bank?" said Angus.

"It's the law," said Olaf.

"But I'm only a novice and I'm going to see it today," said Angus.

"You're now a Sower. Ask the Keeper about it later, When you finish your breakfast I'll take you to the Eye Tower," said Olaf.

"Sounds good," said Angus. He finished off his jam sandwich and washed it down with some pomegranate juice. "Okay. I'm ready."

They went past the Hall of Tree ferns and took a tunnel that twisted upwards. After a few minutes it opened out onto a wide courtyard. At the far end of the courtyard was a three-sided stone tower; a truncated and sleek triangular pyramid.

"The Eye Tower," said Olaf.

They walked up the path to the wooden door and entered the tower. All the walls were lined with ancient books. It was a long climb to the top.

"I'll show you how to find things in this library another time," said Olaf. They walked out onto a stone parapet.

"This is the highest point of the Monastery," said Olaf. One side looked over the Glen of Goats, another faced the Caldera Gardens, the third side looked out to sea. To the northwest the nurseries spread out over the mountains for several kilometres.

Olaf pointed to the northwest and said, "The north-western nurseries are tended by the Brotherhood of Sowers."

He pointed east across the Caldera Gardens, and said, "The eastern nurseries are tended by the Sisterhood of Sowers. Below us, novice Sowers look after the Caldera Gardens. That's where you will work for the next five years," said Olaf.

"Five years working in the fields. I don't think that I'd like that," said Angus.

"You can study at the same time. There is a lot to take in. You will learn the secrets of animals and plants. Come. I want to show you the northern nurseries," said Olaf.

Olaf went back into the tower. Angus followed him down the steps, out of the tower, down the path and back into the tunnels.

By the end of the afternoon Angus had gone through several massive glasshouses built on mountaintops. They were now at the most northern nursery. It was in a high valley that had been roofed over with a tough glass-like substance. To the west was the sea. To the north there were more mountains. The east side of the mountain sloped down to the Caldera Gardens.

Olaf pointed to the mountains in the north.

"The Bog Lands are beyond there," said Olaf.

"That peak across there. Is that Mount Suil?" asked Angus.

"Yes. You can't see the village from here. It's hidden behind those rocks."

Angus looked down into the gardens. He watched the river as it flowed through the valley and then disappeared among the mountains to the north.

"What happens to the river when it reaches the mountains?" asked Angus.

"It flows into a steep gorge and then disappears underground. It must come out in the Bog Lands," said Olaf.

"Have you not explored it?" asked Angus.

"We used to collect rare plants down in the gorge but that was before Brother Torquil went missing down there," said Olaf.

"You didn't find anything?" asked Angus.

"We found his herb basket and a piece of cloth seeped in blood." said Olaf.

"How many others have gone missing?" asked Angus.

"Three. Brother Gareth disappeared first. It was about three months ago. He was working late on a ditch over there near the orchard," said Olaf. He pointed along the river to the start of the orchard.

"Then Brother Torquil disappeared down there in that gorge," said Olaf.

"What about the third person?" asked Angus.

"Oh! Sister Bridgid. That was only two days after Brother Torquil disappeared. We were low on sphagnum moss and sundew so Sister Bridgid made an expedition to the Bog Lands. She never came back," said Olaf.

"Wasn't that a dangerous place to go to with all the graks there?" said Angus.

"The one we met in the Gardens was in heat. They aren't usually aggressive and keep well away from humans. Sister Bridgid had been to the Bog Lands on plenty of excursions before. We sent out a search party but the Bog Lands are treacherous. One wrong slip and you're sucked under. No trace left," said Olaf.

"These graks. If you created them can't you get rid of them, poison them or something?" said Angus.

"We've tried. They are resistant to everything," said Olaf.

"There's the Keeper," said Angus. He pointed to a figure in a purple cloak walking up the steps cut into the mountainside.

"Yes. We'll go down to meet him," said Olaf.

They walked back through the massive glasshouse to a tunnel. It wound down several levels and then opened out into an empty hall with no windows. The Keeper was waiting for them.

"Angus, novice Sower. You are now to visit the seed banks. Follow me," said the Keeper.

He walked down a corridor that ended in a metal door with the torus symbol. The Keeper pressed the symbol and the door opened to reveal a lift. The Keeper walked into the lift and Angus followed. The doors shut and the lift descended.

63

"Why can't Mind Casters see the seed banks," asked Angus. At first the keeper did not say anything and Angus thought his question was going to be ignored. Then he slowly turned to Angus.

The Keeper said, "They were, once. It started a war."

"When? What happened?" asked Angus.

The Keeper sighed and said," It was over a thousand years ago. A Mind Caster named Okkan was not content when he became Head Mind Caster. He was greedy for more power and used his talent to corrupt the seed banks. He created a batch of his own Mind Caster clones and genetically "improved" them through mind manipulation."

"What happened to them?" asked Angus.

"They were finally destroyed by the Storm Hags, but not before they killed hundreds of people," said the Keeper.

The lift stopped and the doors opened onto a plain white room. The Keeper walked into the middle of the room.

"This is the decontamination room. Come into the middle and then cover your eyes for a few seconds. It uses a powerful light," said the Keeper.

Angus moved into the room and shut his eyes. He felt a tingling feeling all over his body and then the Keeper was telling him that he could open his eyes. The Keeper pressed his hand against a white wall and it slid away to reveal a huge chamber hollowed out of the base rock of the mountain. The walls and floors were set out in dark polished stone.

"This is the seed bank. Most of the specimens are minuscule samples held in stasis," said the Keeper. He stepped into the chamber, followed by Angus. To the left and right were long corridors with sealed doors leading off on both sides. Straight in front was a large empty area. At the far end was a raised area, covered by a glass dome. The Keeper walked up to a panel set into the wall. He pressed it and it glowed.

"Press your hand on the scanner. It will creates a master key that responds to your genetic code," said the Keeper.

Angus spread his hand out on the panel. It tingled as his hand was scanned.

"You can open most doors in the seed bank now. Come, I'll show you around" said the Keeper.

They walked down the corridor on the right hand side. The sealed doors were coded with writing that Angus had not seen before. The Keeper stopped at a door and pressed it. The door slid open. The room was very cold and Angus shivered. The Keeper pressed a white wall and it became transparent. Out of swirling mist a woolly mammoth with wicked tusks peered down at them.

Angus jumped back.

"This room contain full size specimen samples from the animal kingdom," said the Keeper.

"Cool. Where did you dig it up from? I've heard of them being found in Siberia in the permafrost," said Angus.

"This creature was not dug up. It is living. It's in stasis," said the Keeper.

"You mean it's alive. In some kind of suspended animation?" asked Angus.

The Keeper shook his head. He said, "Alive, yes. Suspended animation, no. That's no use when we are thinking in thousands of years."

"How?" asked Angus.

"Good questions from a novice Sower. Say I put you in suspended animation. Your heart is still beating, very slowly, but still beating. Eventually it would run down. When you were woken up in a thousand years time your heart would rapidly deteriorate. Understand?" said the Keeper.

"I think so," said Angus.

"So we use a method called stasis. Everything is completely stopped," said the Keeper. He pressed on the transparent wall and it became opaque.

"You have a try," said the Keeper.

Angus looked around the room. There was nothing to help him know what was where. He pressed a wall at random. A small part of the wall became transparent. Angus recognized the creature from drawings in books. It was a Dodo. The extinct bird stared blankly back at Angus.

"On special occasions we create a batch of them. There's nothing like Dodo pie," said the Keeper. He licked his lips. "In fact I'll start off a batch now. We can celebrate your joining the Sowers. Right, watch me now. We're just going to make an ordinary batch of clones." The Keeper pointed to some symbols on the wall below the dodo. There was a simple outline of a dodo, a torus and a triangle.

"There are two ways to do this. You can use the symbols here to directly input the batch amount or you can do it from the database in the control room. If you need to do a lot at once or some gene splicing the control room's best," said the Keeper. He pressed the dodo once and then the torus three times.

"That should be enough. The batch should be ready in ten minutes time," said the Keeper.

"How will they be ready so quickly?" asked Angus.

"In built mortality gene. Makes them age fast," said the Keeper.

"Do you clone people in the same way?" asked Angus.

"The method is the same. Of course we don't put in a mortality gene in human clones," said the Keeper.

"You mean that the human clones will live forever?" asked Angus.

The Keeper sighed, "No. I mean that human clones are aged at a normal rate. We tried to speed up development. It had disastrous results."

"So what happened?" asked Angus.

"Their minds couldn't stand it. They all went mad and died after a few days," said the Keeper. "Come. I'll show you how the human clones are grown."

The Keeper went out of the room and walked further down the corridor. He pressed another door. It opened out into a long narrow room. Down one wall was a row of tall glass cylinders filled with a green bubbling liquid. Figures floated in the cylinders.

"These are the development vats. After the clones are removed from the artificial wombs they are each allocated a vat," said the Keeper.

The Keeper stopped at the first cylinder. A boy, slightly younger than Angus, floated in the liquid. His eyes were shut. There were tubes coming from around his body and wires protruding from his head.

"The tubes supply the clone with nutrition and also remove waste products. The wires stimulate the brain cells. We find this the most efficient method of teaching," said the Keeper.

"So how long are they kept in these vats?" asked Angus.

"Usually the clone is decanted when it has reached ten years. By then the brain has been correctly wired and prepared for external stimulus," said the Keeper.

"I wonder if he dreams?" said Angus. He looked at the boy's face.

The Keeper shrugged and said, "It didn't do me any harm. Come. It's time to go back to the Grand Hall. I will show you more tomorrow."

The Keeper went out of the door and down the corridor. Angus followed him to the main room. There were three small dodos running around in the glass dome. The Keeper went up to the control panel and pressed a couple of symbols. A pink gas hissed into the glass dome and everything was obscured. After a few seconds the gas was sucked out. The three dodos were out lying flat on the floor of the dome. There was a mechanical noise and the dome lifted up. The Keeper picked up the birds and held them by the feet.

Angus had seen documentaries of how chickens were killed in factories. He knew that animals were killed so that he could eat but the easy quickness of it all made him feel sick. He followed the Keeper back into the decontamination room and into the lift. He did not try to have another conversation with the Keeper and kept silent all the way back to the Grand Hall. Angus's stomach made a gurgling sound. He was very hungry. He looked at the three dead dodos. Their head swung back and

66

fore as the Keeper carried them. Six dead eyes stared blankly at him. Angus wondered if they would taste like chicken or be greasier like a goose.

The Apprentice

Kirsty was dreaming that she was a bird flying high in the sky. She looked down and saw a frozen sea stretching for kilometres in every direction. She didn't know where to go and she was also feeling tired. She heard a light voice calling to her.

"Kirsty!" said the voice. Kirsty woke up to see Lady Morgana bent over her with a concerned expression on her face. She touched Kirsty's forehead with cool fingers.

"You don't seem to have a fever but your temperature's up. How are you feeling?" asked Lady Morgana.

Kirsty sat up in bed and the memories of the Temple of Suil came rushing back.

"I'm fine. Where's Angus?" said Kirsty.

"Don't worry about your brother. Olaf is out teaching him how to be a Sower," smiled Lady Morgana. She held out a blue robe. "Here's your new robe. You can get rid of that grey thing now. I'm here to help you become a Mind Caster. "

"I don't know about that. That test was kinda scary," said Kirsty. She took the robe. It felt lovely and soft like silk.

"You have a powerful gift and we may have need of it," said Lady Morgana.

"What do you mean?" asked Kirsty.

Lady Morgana walked across the room and opened the bedroom door. She looked out into the corridor. Satisfied she came back in and shut the door.

"I've got this feeling that I'm being watched. There is something evil going on. Something that is getting more powerful by the day. I fear for Gruinsoye," said Lady Morgana.

"The Storm Hags said that too," said Kirsty.

Lady Morgana took a soft leather pouch from her cloak. She handed it to Kirsty.

"This is your own scrying stone. The Storm Hags had their ravens deliver it especially," said Lady Morgana. "I'll show you some mind exercises."

Kirsty opened the pouch and took out the stone. It was grey with a light blue crackled pattern like tiny veins. The stone glowed slightly as she touched it.

"Hold it like this in yours hands," said Lady Morgana. She took her own stone from around her neck and held it flat out in her palms. Kirsty did the same.

"First you'll have to find out how to tune into your stone. For example, I image myself as a tiny ant. I imagine that I am walking along the inner hole of the torus. The stone stretches out above and behind me and I start to run. I then run faster and faster," said Lady Morgana. The stone rose from her palm and started to spin on its axis.

"The stone rotating is its default charging state. See if you can do that," said Lady Morgana. She let her stone drop back into her palm.

Kirsty tried thinking of herself as an ant walking along the inner edge of the stone.

"I can't do it. I don't know how it worked with Kallid's stone," said Kirsty.

"He's trained his stone so it was probably helping you. You see the training works both ways," said Lady Morgana.

"You mean that the stone is alive?" asked Kirsty.

"Yes, in a way," said Morgana.

Kirsty tried to think of herself as an ant again. She screwed up her face.

"It's not working. I don't like ants," said Kirsty.

"Oh, it doesn't have to be an ant. Anything that makes you aware of dimensions and speed," said Lady Morgana.

Kirsty stared at the stone again. She thought of her dream as a bird. She imagined she was a tiny bird flying over a huge curved mountain. She flapped her wings and she flew faster and faster. The scrying stone glowed and rose from her hand. It started to rotate above her hand.

"Good. Keep doing that. Now I'm going to use my mind to push the stone towards you. I want you to try and keep it," said Lady Morgana.

Kirsty felt a light tug on the stone. It started to move towards Lady Morgana. Kirsty imagined the stone back on her palm. The stone moved about ten centimetres then remained, rotating in the air.

Lady Morgana said, "Have you ever gone fishing?"

"Yes. I go with Angus. He threads the worm on the hook for me," said Kirsty.

"Imaging casting out your line. Do it with your mind. Cast out to the stone," said Lady Morgana.

Kirsty imagined having a fishing rod in her hands. She felt the weight of the rod as she drew it back, then swept it forward, the imaginary hook and sinker hitting the stone.

"Now reel it in," said Lady Morgana.

Kirsty imagined the hook catching on the stone. She reeled it in with her mind. The stone floated back towards her and stopped just above her palm, rotating slowly.

Lady Morgana laughed and said, "You've really got the hang of it. It took me a long time to learn to pull or push the stone. Now let's see what's your precognition level. Keep looking into the stone."

Kirsty looked at the stone spinning around in front of her eyes. It was hypnotic.

Lady Morgana said, "Keep looking at the stone as it spins. You should be able to make out an eye shape?"

"Yes, I can see it. It's all blurry though," said Kirsty in an excited voice.

"Now that you've got the eye shape imagine that it is wrapping around your head. You can see in all directions at once. Different points of light fly past you," said Lady Morgana.

"I can't see that at all. I can't imagine seeing in all directions at once," said Kirsty.

"Okay. Concentrate on the eye shape. Bring your mind closer to the black hole; the pupil. Can you do that?" said Lady Morgana.

"Okay I'm looking through the pupil. I can't see anything," said Kirsty.

"Not even a shadow. A dark blue against black?" asked Lady Morgana.

"No, nothing," said Kirsty. The stone slowed down its rotation and gently landed on Kirsty's outstretched palm.

"I don't think you even meet level one on precognition. I thought because of your telekinetic power that maybe, oh never mind," said Lady Morgana.

"What level are you?" asked Kirsty.

"I'm a level three. I can see certain events in detail and other things are vague," said Lady Morgana.

"Can you see anything now?" asked Kirsty.

"For the past few months all I've seen is mist and bogs," said Lady Morgana.

"Do you think that means something?" asked Kirsty.

"I often see mist but not usually bogs. This is more like someone is trying to hide something from me," said Lady Morgana. "I'll try again."

She held out her palm and concentrated on the stone. It rose up into the air and began to rotate. Kirsty watched Lady Morgana's face go slack as she went into a trance. The pupils on her eyes grew huge. She remained in that position for around twenty seconds and then her pupils went back to normal. The stone stopped rotating and landed on her hand.

Lady Morgana said, "It's the same vision again. I'm walking on a path. It must be the Bog Lands. A mist is coming down. There are the sounds of graks all around me. I can feel something is watching me. Something hideous and evil that wishes to do me harm." Lady Morgana shuddered. Kirsty gave her a hug. Lady Morgana was surprised but smiled and gave Kirsty a hug back.

"I'm sure it's to do with Sister Bridgid's disappearance. It's been weighing on my mind," sighed Lady Morgana.

"Who was she?" said Kirsty.

"Bridgid was my batch sister although she didn't pass the Mind Caster test. Poor Bridgid," said Lady Morgana.

"Did she disappear like the Brothers. Olaf said something about it," said Kirsty.

"She went to the Bog Lands to stock up on some plants. She asked me to accompany her. I was too busy. I should have gone. That was the last time I saw her," said Lady Morgana.

"Was there a search party?" asked Kirsty.

"Soyean led it. They found nothing," said Lady Morgana. She wiped her eyes, stood up and went over to the window. She looked out to sea.

"Kirsty!"

There was a knock on the bedroom door. Lady Morgana went over and opened it.

"Kirsty I, Oh it's you!" said Angus.

Lady Morgana smiled as she moved out of the way to let Angus into the room. She turned to Kirsty.

"I think that you've done enough for today. Go through your mind exercises a couple of times before you go to sleep. I'll come and see you tomorrow. Angus don't keep your sister up too long. She's still weak," said Lady Morgana.

"I won't. Goodnight," said Angus.

"Goodnight," said Lady Morgana.

"Goodnight," said Kirsty. Lady Morgana closed the door. Angus came and sat on the bed beside Kirsty.

"How are you feeling?" asked Angus.

"I'm a bit tired but see what Lady Morgana brought me," said Kirsty. She held out her scrying stone.

"Cool. Does it work like Kallid's one?" asked Angus.

"Yes. Watch this!" said Kirsty as she concentrated on the stone. The stone floated up out of her palm and started to rotate. It stopped and fell back into her palm.

"I'm too tired now. I need to go to sleep. Can you shut the curtains for me?" said Kirsty.

"Don't you want to know about the seed banks?" asked Angus

71

"Tell me tomorrow Angus. I'm really tired," said Kirsty. She yawned. Angus got up and went over to the window. He drew the curtains.

"You'll never guess what we're going to have for dinner?" said Angus.

Kirsty didn't answer. Angus turned around. Kirsty was fast asleep. Angus went over to the bed. He took the stone out of her hand and put it in the soft leather pouch beside the bed. He pulled the blankets up around Kirsty and tucked her in.

"Goodnight. You're missing out on dodo pie," said Angus. He put out the light and left the bedroom.

Kidnapped

Angus woke up. There was a familiar smell in the room. He sat bolt upright. That was the smell of a grak! He pulled a robe on and rushed to Kirsty's bedroom. The windows were wide open and moonlight flooded the room. The bed was empty and the covers were in a heap on the floor. He heard a scream from far below.

"Angus!"

Angus ran to the window and looked down. It was still quite dark but he could make out shadows crawling down the cliff face, towards the sea. They seemed to disappear at the foot of the cliff.

"Kirsty!" he shouted.

A chorus of clicking noises came up from below, and then all Angus could hear was the crashing of waves.

He ran through to the Grand Hall and pressed his hand against the symbol on the door. The door did not open. He tried banging it with his fist. There was no sound at all. It was as if the door swallowed up the vibrations. He looked at the circle within a circle symbol embossed on the door. It looked like the torus shape of the scrying stone belonging to Kallid. Angus touched the symbol and thought of the scrying stone. He imagined it in the air in front of him. The door slid open and the Keeper entered.

"The graks have taken Kirsty!" said Angus.

"What? Talk sense! " said the Keeper.

"It's true. Come and see for yourself!" said Angus.

He pulled at the Keeper's hand. The Keeper pulled his hand away.

"Constrain yourself," he said. He followed Angus into Kirsty's bedroom.

"See," said Angus. He pointed to the empty bed.

The Keeper looked around the room. He slowly bent down and looked under the bed. He groaned as he straightened his back. He pushed through the pile of sheets with his staff, fished out one of the sheets and pointed out a dark stain.

"Blood!" said the Keeper.

"Oh no!" said Angus

The Keeper moved over to the window and looked out. It was dawn and he could see the waves crashing against the foot of the cliff below. Angus came and stood beside the Keeper at the window.

Angus pointed to the foot of the cliff and said, "I saw them climbing down to the bottom of the cliff. Then they disappeared."

The Keeper looked at him and scratched his head. "If I remember rightly there is a cave entrance down there. The graks are good climbers but to come all the way up here and then kidnap the female?" The Keeper went into the Grand Hall and sat down.

Angus came through and said, "I have to get my sister back. I must get to that cave!"

I didn't think they have much intelligence. It sounds like they were guided by someone or something else," said the Keeper.

"Where does that cave lead to?" asked Angus.

The door slid open and Olaf came in. He saw Angus's face and knew something was wrong.

"The graks have taken Kirsty," said Angus.

"Graks, here?" said Olaf.

"Yes. They somehow climbed the cliff and snatched her while I was sleeping. Then I saw them with her at the bottom of the cliff," said Angus.

"There is a cave mouth," said The Keeper. "It is said to lead under the mountains to the Bog Lands."

"It must be part of the same network of tunnels that the river disappears into from the Caldera Gardens. I don't know how to get in there," said Olaf.

"It's strange that the graks would go to all that trouble," said the Keeper. He stroked his beard and frowned.

"It does sounds too complicated a plan for graks?" said Olaf.

"There's something evil behind all this," said the Keeper.

"The Storm Hags said something about that too," said Angus.

"It must be linked to the disappearances. First Brother Gareth disappears three months ago and then last month Brother Torquil and Sister Bridgid," said the Keeper.

Angus suddenly had an idea and said," How about my liferaft. It's still at the beach. We could row around and get to the cave that way!"

Olaf shook his head and said, "It's too dangerous. There are too many rocks around the cliff. If you weren't smashed by the rocks the Corriekraken Whirlpool would get you."

"Well what about getting some ropes and abseiling down the cliff?" said Angus.

"Abseiling?" asked Olaf.

"Holding onto the rope and using the face of the cliff to walk down. You wear a belt with a metal loop through it to let out the rope and you go down," said Angus.

"Yes. We use something similar to collect bird's eggs from the cliffs," said Olaf.

The Keeper said, "I will arrange to get the ropes. You will need weapons and torches. Olaf, you have my authority to collect frosticks from the armoury."

Olaf, Angus and the Keeper left the Grand Hall. They walked through the Hall of Ferns and down the tunnel. The Keeper went off down a tunnel to the right and Olaf took a smaller tunnel. Angus followed Olaf. They eventually came to a steel door set in the wall. Olaf pressed it and entered. The room was like a bunker; all the walls were made of metal. Strange instruments lay in clear plastic boxes on shelves. Olaf opened a box and took out three tubes. He tucked two of them into his cloak and gave the third one to Angus.

"Come out into the corridor and I'll show you how to use them!" said Olaf.

Angus followed Olaf out into the corridor. The steel door closed behind them.

"Be careful. This is a frostick. See these three blue dots?" said Olaf. He took the weapon from Angus and turned it around in his hands. It was made of a light metal and was hollow. Olaf pointed out three blue dots etched into the metal near one end.

"Yes," said Angus.

"Always have the end with the dots closest to you. Hold it in your hand like this." He held the frostick out. "Aim, then press down three times quickly on the dots, like so."

Olaf aimed at the rock wall of the corridor. He pressed quickly down on the dots. There was a green flash and the wall was covered in a thick layer of ice.

"Cool!" said Angus.

Olaf gave him back the frostick and said, "You have a go!"

Angus aimed the frostick at another wall and pressed three times. A flash of green light came from the end of the tube and the wall was covered in ice.

"You've got the hang of it. Let's get back to the Grand Hall," said Olaf.

They walked quickly to the Grand Hall. The Keeper was there with another man.

"This is Wilfred. He's our best egg gatherer. He will accompany you," said the Keeper.

Wilfred was small and skinny, with long blond hair and a hooked nose. He nodded towards Angus.

"Here take these glow globes. You'll need some light in that cave. There's enough charge in each to last about two hours on full power," said the Keeper. He gave each of them a sphere made of a light white material. They were about the size of a tennis ball and had a ridge running around its circumference.

"We must secure the ropes," said Wilfred.

Olaf and Wilfred gathered up several piles of ropes and went into Kirsty's bedroom. Wilfred looked out the window.

"The cave's at the bottom of the cliff," said Angus.

Wilfred nodded. He looked around the window frame. There was nothing there to tie the ropes to.

"How about the bed?" said Olaf. "It's heavy and made of metal. We could tie the ropes to its legs and wedge it under the windowsill."

"Yes, that would work. Help me lift it over to the window," said Wilfred.

Olaf and Wilfred dragged the bed over to the window. They jammed it lengthways under the windowsill. Wilfred tied ropes to the base of the bed with complicated knots. He pulled on a rope to test it.

"Put these harnesses on!" said Wilfred. He held out leather harnesses to Olaf and Angus. "Make sure that the metal hoop is in front of your stomach."

Olaf and Angus buckled into their harnesses. Wilfred checked them. He tightened Angus's harness.

"Now do as I do. Take this end of the rope and pull it through the loop. Hitch it around once, like this," said Wilfred.

Angus and Olaf did as he asked.

Wilfred said, "Good. Now you are able to control how much rope to let out and hence how far to descend." He got up onto the window ledge. He threw the rope down. It uncoiled and fell down the face of the cliff. Wilfred took up the slack and lent back out of the window. He slowly stepped out of the window. He was now at an angle to the cliff face. He started to walk down the cliff, letting the rope out slowly.

"Right, you two can start coming down now," he shouted.

Angus was scared out of his wits but he got up onto the windowsill and let the rope out. He did the same as Wilfred and started to abseil down the cliff. Olaf followed after him. It was slow going. There were many crevasses and jutting out ledges to navigate. About half way down a guillemot flew from a ledge squawking. It startled Angus. He slipped and fell several metres before he managed to pull tightly on the loop on the rope.

Olaf came down beside him and asked, "Are you alright?"

"I've scratched my knee and elbow but I'm okay," said Angus. "Just give me a minute. My heart is banging against my rib cage."

Olaf abseiled down the cliff slowly, next to Angus. Wilfred was waiting anxiously at the cave mouth, which was a few metres above the crashing waves. Angus and Olaf finally got level with Wilfred without any further mishap.

"You okay Angus?" shouted Wilfred over the noise of the crashing waves. He held onto Angus's rope and pulled him into the cave.

"Yes thanks. Just skinned my knee," shouted Angus.

Olaf swung into the cave. They unbuckled themselves from the ropes and took off their harnesses. Angus looked around the damp dark entrance. The floor of the cave was covered in a layer of slippery seaweed and the place smelled of rotten fish.

"That smell! Phew!" shouted Angus. He put his hand over his nose.

"You better have this," shouted Olaf. He gave Wilfred a frostick. "Right. Angus, this is how you use the glow globes." Olaf held out the sphere in his palm. He pressed his other palm on top of the sphere and twisted it clockwise. There was a clicking noise and the sphere started to glow. Light flooded the cave and giant shadows were cast against the walls.

"The more you twist it, the more light is emitted," shouted Olaf.

Angus and Wilfred got out their glow globes and twisted them up to the full setting. About ten metres into the cave there was a dark opening.

"I better go first," shouted Wilfred. He walked carefully across the slippery floor of the cave to the entrance of the passage. He disappeared around a corner.

"Wait for us!" cried out Angus.

"You stay in the middle," said Olaf. He let Angus past him, and then they hurried after Wilfred. The passage sloped upwards and was still wet, but it was now free of seaweed. They walked along the passage for several minutes, the sound of the crashing waves got weaker and weaker until Angus didn't know if he could still hear them or it was just the sound of blood rushing through his ears. Wilfred had stopped further up. Angus and Olaf caught up with him. The passage had split into two tunnels.

"Which way now?" asked Wilfred.

Olaf went a few metres into the left tunnel and sniffed the air. He came back then went up the right tunnel for a few metres.

"The left one smells of grak, I think," he said.

"Okay," said Wilfred. He led the way up the left tunnel. After about twenty metres he stopped, bent down and picked something up off the ground. Angus and Olaf came up beside him. Wilfred held out a stone torus. He handed it to Angus.

"It's a scrying stone," gasped Angus. "It must be Kirsty's. We're on the right track." Angus put it into a pocket in the folds of his cloak.

They carried on up the tunnel. After a few minutes it started to level out and the walls began to glow with a greenish tint. Angus touched the wall. Green glowing slime came off in his hand. Olaf stopped and looked back at Angus.

"What've you found?" asked Olaf.

77

"Oh nothing. I just wondered what this goo was," replied Angus. He held out his glowing hand.

"It's a type of luminous algae," said Olaf. He twisted his glow globe off. "Turn your glow globe off," he said. Angus twisted off his globe.

Wilfred stopped and said, "What are you up to?"

"Wilfred. Turn you globe off," said Olaf.

Wilfred turned off his glow globe and they were plunged into darkness. In a few seconds their eyes adjusted and the darkness gave way to a green glow.

"It's like wearing green sunglasses," said Angus as he looked around the tunnel.

"It will save the power in the glow globes. We might need them later," said Olaf.

"Good idea," said Wilfred.

They carried on walking along the tunnel and after about half an hour they started to hear a rushing noise. They went round a corner and the tunnel opened out into a huge cathedral like cavern. Stalactites hung down like ornate gothic chandeliers from the high roof. From a few hundred metres to the left a murky river flowed from a low arch in the cave wall. It was half hidden in places as it meandered between pillars formed by the meeting of stalactites and stalagmites. The river curved past them and emptied into a vast underground lake that stretched away into the distance.

"The Loch of the Golden Harp," gasped Wilfred.

"That's only a legend," said Olaf shaking his head.

"Are you sure?" said Wilfred. Olaf shrugged his shoulders.

They walked beside the river to where it fed into the loch.

"I don't like this place. It gives me the creeps," said Angus.

"I can't see any other tunnels. They must have taken Kirsty across it," said Olaf.

Angus stared at his eerie green reflection in the dark water. "I don't fancy swimming in that."

"Maybe there's something we could use as a raft. Spread out. Let's have a look around. Wilfred, you look along the right side of the loch! Angus you stay here and I'll walk back alongside the river to where it comes in here!" said Olaf.

"You must be joking. I'm not staying here by myself," shivered Angus. "I'll stick with you."

"Alright. Come on then," said Olaf.

Wilfred set off to the right and Angus followed Olaf back along the bank of the river.

Not long past the tunnel they came to a set of pillars. When they walked around behind them they came across a wooden jetty. Two tiny oval boats were tied up to it.

"Eureka!" said Angus. He walked along the short jetty and bent down to look at the canoes.

"They look as if they're made from leather," said Angus.

Olaf came onto the jetty. He stepped down into the nearest boat. It displaced a lot of water but stayed afloat.

"Seems safe enough. But doesn't hold much weight. We'll have to use both of them. A single boat would not take the weight of all three of us," said Olaf. He got out of the boat and back onto the jetty.

"I better test the other one," he said. Olaf got into the other boat and sat down. It seemed watertight but was only about six centimetres above the surface of the river. He untied the boat from the jetty and pushed off into the river.

"Come on we'll pick Wilfred up," Olaf said.

Angus got into the other boat, untied it and pushed off from the jetty. The little oval boat was supplied with a wooden paddle. Angus spun round a couple of times before he got the hang of steering with it. They drifted with the current down the river and out onto the loch.

"Wilfred," shouted Olaf. His voice echoed across the loch.

"Hello," shouted back Wilfred.

"There he is," said Angus. "Look he's standing on that boulder over there." They paddled towards Wilfred.

"Where did you find the boats?" asked Wilfred as Olaf and Angus drew alongside the boulder.

"Up near where the river flows into the cavern," said Olaf.

"There's a wee jetty," said Angus.

Wilfred made as if to step into the boat with Olaf.

"I think you better go in with Angus. These boats don't hold much weight and I'm much heavier than you," said Olaf.

Angus steered his boat closer and Wilfred got aboard. The boat was about ten centimetres above the surface of the loch.

"Are we okay?" asked Olaf.

"Fine," said Angus.

"I think I can see a shore away across the loch. We'll head for that," said Olaf.

"I'll row if you like," said Wilfred.

"It's okay. I'll let you have a shot when I'm tired," said Angus with a determined look on his face. Wilfred shrugged his shoulders. Angus used the paddle to push off from the boulder. He paddled out into the loch after Olaf. Angus was quite tired and would have liked to let Wilfred take over but he still had an eerie feeling. He thought that paddling would take his mind off the terrible foreboding that pressed down on him. The hairs on the back of his neck stood up as he looked around the loch. There were bunches of strange plants here and there.

In the distance they seemed to be covering the loch like some weird underworld waterlily.

Wilfred's voice startled him.

"Isn't it amazing," said Wilfred.

"What?" asked Angus.

"Look over there at the stalactites reflected in the water," said Wilfred. The boat passed a clump of floating purple and pink flowers. The heads were the sizes of footballs.

"I've never seen such waterlilies," said Wilfred.

Angus said, "I think they're creepy."

"It's a magical place," said Wilfred.

"When we were children our batch nurse used to tell us the story of The Loch of the Golden Harp," said Wilfred.

"What kind of story?" asked Angus.

"The story starts with a magic golden harp. Anyone who played it could bring the dead back to life."

"Cool! Like a zombie?" asked Angus.

"I don't know," said Wilfred.

"Go on," said Angus.

"This King's daughter died and he was so sorry. He sent his most trusted soldier to fetch the harp. Now, the harp was kept in a temple on an island. This island was in the middle of a huge underground lake called The Loch of the Golden Harp,"

"Like this one? But I can't see an island anywhere?" said Angus.

"Yes but that was the thing. The island moved from day to day so that when.. Hey! My feet are wet."

Angus looked down. Water was starting to come into the boat. He looked around the cavern. The nearest shore was quite far off.

"Olaf. We're bringing water in!" shouted Wilfred. Olaf turned his boat around.

Wilfred felt along the bottom of the boat.

He said, "I've found where the water is coming in. I'll try and bung it up. Make for the nearest shore."

Wilfred held his hands over the hole and Angus paddled as fast as he could towards the shore. Olaf came along side.

"It's not working!" said Wilfred, "Angus get in with Olaf."

Angus clambered out of the sinking boat. The boat got dangerously low down in the water when Angus got in with Olaf. Wilfred paddled as fast as he could towards the shore but the boat continued to fill up. Wilfred jumped from the boat and swam for the shore. There was a rushing noise from further down the loch as something large moved under the water. There was a flash of sharp needle like teeth and a grey snout and the sinking boat was pulled sharply under.

"Wilfred. Swim as fast as you can!" shouted Olaf as he paddled towards the beach.

Wilfred turned his head around and saw the boat being dragged under the water. He swam as fast as he could. He imagined jaws snapping at his heels as he swam through the black water of the loch. Something caught his leg.

"Arrgh," screamed Wilfred. He kicked his leg loose. It was stuck on weed. He scrambled up onto the shore.

Angus and Olaf paddled up. Wilfred helped them pull the boat up onto the shore.

There was a splashing noise as something large twisted round in the water then swam back down to the depths.

"What was that?" asked Angus.

"I never want to find out," said Wilfred.

They sat on the shore and rested for a while. They had travelled so far down the loch that they could no longer see the river mouth. A narrow shore stretched into the distance in the opposite direction.

"I don't fancy going back into the water," said Wilfred.

"There's not enough room for all of us in one boat anyway," said Angus.

"We'll follow the shoreline. It's in the right direction," said Olaf.

They got up and made their way along the shore. As they walked along, the loch became more congested with the strange underworld waterlilies. Other plants started to appear. Angus recognized one plant as a large version of sphagnum moss. A mist crept in around them. It was so thick that they could only see several metres in front of themselves.

"Angus hold onto the end of Wilfred's cloak. I'll hold onto your cloak. We don't want to lose each other in this mist," said Olaf.

They moved in a line, holding onto each other's cloaks. After they had walked for another ten minutes Olaf said, "Can you feel that warm wind?"

"Yes. Coming from the left?" said Wilfred.

"I think it must be an exit from the caves," said Olaf.

"We don't know which way they took Kirsty," said Angus.

"There's a smell of graks in that wind. Find the graks and you find Kirsty. Head into that wind," said Olaf.

They walked in single file through the ghostly white mist, towards the source of the wind. After a few minutes the mist cleared slightly. Angus looked up and saw twinkling lights.

"I can see the stars. We're out of the caves," said Angus.

Olaf looked around and said, "We've come out in the Bog Lands. Everyone watch out where you stand!"

81

The clicking noise of graks echoed over the marsh as the smell of rotting fish got stronger.

The Cloned Seer

Kirsty woke up with a thumping headache. She tried to sit up but found that her wrists and ankles were held down with clamps to a metal chair. She tried to struggle but the clamps were too tight. She looked around the room. It was some kind of laboratory. On her left were shelves and bottles. Strange machines with flashing lights hung from the ceiling. She looked towards her right. A boy floated upright in a tall glass cylinder filled with green bubbling liquid. His eyes were shut and cables were attached to parts of his body. He was the boy she had seen before in her dreams. Behind the cylinder was a bank of control panels.

"Hello!" shouted Kirsty.

The boy did not seem to hear her. She shouted again.

"Can you hear me?"

Kirsty heard the noise of a door open behind her. She twisted her neck to look round. "Ah. So you're awake", said a voice. Kirsty thought that she recognized it.

"Soyean!" shouted Kirsty.

Soyean walked round the table and smiled into Kirsty's face.

"Untie me. What do you think you're up to!" said Kirsty.

"I need you for a little experiment," said Soyean.

"Like that boy there. What have you done to him?" asked Kirsty.

"Now that I have you he is surplus to my needs," said Soyean.

"I demand that you release me at once!" shouted Kirsty.

"Hush now child. You're hardly in a position to make demands," said Soyean.

"What's the meaning of this? The Keeper and Lady Morgana will be furious!" shouted Kirsty.

"Help me. Help, anyone!" she shouted. Kirsty struggled to pull her wrists from the clamps.

"There's no use struggling and you can scream all you want. There's no one to help you," said Soyean.

"Help. Anyone!" shouted Kirsty. Soyean came up to Kirsty and yawned in her face.

"I'm getting a trifle bored with your outbursts," said Soyean. "As I said before there is no one to help you. If you persist I will have to gag you."

"Angus will look for me. He'll get help. Wait and see," said Kirsty.

"A mere boy. Pah!" tutted Soyean. "Besides I'm not going to hurt you. I just need you to help with some of my experiments and then you are free to go."

"What kind of experiments? Let me out of this and I'll think about helping you," said Kirsty.

"Gruinsoye is in decline. We have the technology of the old ones and what happens? The Keeper is the only one with access to it. An ancient decrepit old man. He has no ambition. Lady Morgana dotes on him. She is also weak. Two hundred centuries ago Gruinsoye ruled the world, and so it will again."

"So what's that got to do with me?" asked Kirsty.

"You have been sent to me to help with my mind boosting experiments. It is my destiny to become ruler of Gruinsoye," said Soyean.

"You're mad. Why do you think that I would help you?" said Kirsty.

"I have my spies in the Monastery. A simple accident may easily befall your brother. You know the damage a loose stone from a great height can do," said Soyean. Kirsty gasped.

"What do you want from me?" said Kirsty.

"I've managed to perform some of my own cloning experiments. I've not had access to the Keepers knowledge but the outside world has caught up in many aspects. I was able to, what do you outsiders call it, hack in, to research sites on your Internet. As I did not have access to the seed banks it was necessary to kidnap several specimens for experimentation," said Soyean.

"You mean the Brothers that disappeared? I thought it was graks?" said Kirsty.

"Yes. I have the graks under my control. From Brother Gareth I was able to clone this boy. They are from the Brahan Seer stock," said Soyean. He tapped on the glass cylinder.

The boy's eyes opened and stared blankly. "I spliced in a mortality gene to speed up his development but it's not worked. His mind is feeble. I need to create stronger minds to build my new world," said Soyean.

"So where is Brother Gareth and the others?" asked Kirsty.

"Oh I couldn't let them go. They'd tell the Keeper and I'm not ready yet," said Soyean.

"And I'm to believe that you'd let me go?" said Kirsty.

"But you want to leave Gruinsoye. I can arrange for you and your brother to escape this island," said Soyean.

"I don't trust you," said Kirsty.

Soyean smiled, went over to a table and picked up a box. He took out a syringe and came back over to Kirsty. He rolled up her arm and rubbed it with cotton wool and some liquid.

"What are you doing?" asked Kirsty.

"Don't worry. I just need a sample of your blood," said Soyean.

Kirsty turned her face away as he put the needle into her arm. Soyean drew blood into the syringe and then removed the needle.

"There. All done," said Soyean. He put a plaster over the small mark on Kirsty's arm.

Soyean walked across the laboratory. He brought down a box from a shelf and opened it. Inside the box were rows of small glass test tubes filled with green liquid. Carefully he dripped a drop of blood into each of the test tubes.

"What are you doing?" asked Kirsty.

"I'm setting up a few batches of clones of you," said Soyean.

"Why?" asked Kirsty.

"Then I will have your telekinetic powers multifold, all under my control," replied Soyean.

"What for?" asked Kirsty.

"I need more power. I am already much more powerful than Lady Morgana. She got to be chosen Head Mind Caster over me by that senile old Keeper. They do not suspect that my mind experiments have boosted my mental power several times over. Only the Storm Hags are in my way now," said Soyean.

"You destroy others to increase your power. You're a monster," said Kirsty.

"You're boring me again," said Soyean. "I'll speak to you later. I need to try out some fast development experiments on the first batch. Don't go anywhere will you." He laughed and walked towards the door. She heard the door shut behind her. Kirsty felt thirsty and hungry. She looked around the room for some way of escape. There didn't seem to be anything within reach that she could use to help her.

"What about my scrying stone?" Kirsty said to herself.

She then remembered being carried through tunnels by the graks. She remembered it falling from her hand. Kirsty felt her headache coming back. It throbbed in her head like a beating drum. Kirsty looked across at the boy in the cylinder. He blinked his eyes at her. She felt a picture dropping into her mind. It was of the sun. The boy was saying hello. Then she saw another sun. The first sun and the second sun came together and became a larger sun. Kirsty wasn't sure what the boy was trying to say.

"You can put images into my head. You're a telepath?" The boy smiled.

"Who are you?" asked Kirsty. The boy blinked his eyes again. An image of the Seer being dragged up the hill to the fire came into her head.

"The dream," said Kirsty. The boy nodded again.

"I have to call you something. I can't just call you boy or clone," said Kirsty. The boy shrugged.

The Seer's name was Kenneth so I'll call you Kenny," said Kirsty. The boy nodded.

"So Kenny, can you help us get out of here?" Kirsty said. The boy blinked at her. An image of a lock came into her mind. It was a three dimensional image of the locks around her wrist. She could move round the lock as if it was an object in a computer game. She saw where a metal pin had to be moved. She imagined the pin moving and she heard a clicking sound come from the clamps. Her hands were free. A three dimensional image of the locks around her ankles appeared in her head. Again she moved a metal pin with her mind. Her legs were free. Kirsty got up from the chair.

"How can I get you out?" she asked Kenny. An image of a lever flashed into her mind. She looked around the laboratory. Cables from the top of the cylinder ran into a tall machine. Kirsty looked at the dials and controls around the machine. She found the lever and pulled it. There was a hissing sound and the cylinder started to drain. The green liquid gurgled away as the boy pulled cables off his body. There was an unlocking noise and the glass cylinder walls retracted into the ceiling. Kenny stepped onto the floor. He smiled at Kirsty but he was shaking.

"Hold on. I'll find you something to wear," said Kirsty. She looked around the room and picked up a lab coat from a bench. She gave it to Kenny and he put it on.

"Are you okay?" asked Kirsty. The boy nodded.

"We have to get away from here. Do you know the way?" said Kirsty. Kenny shook his head. She tried the door. It was locked.

"Can we try the lock on the door?" said Kirsty. Kenny nodded. They stared at the door and imagined the lock in three-dimensional space. With their combined telekinetic power the lock was quickly opened and the door sprung open. Kirsty looked out into the corridor. It was empty.

"Come on!" said Kirsty. They walked out into the long dim corridor. Grey rock walls stretched out in either direction. There was a sound of footsteps coming from the right side of the corridor.

"Let's go this way!" said Kirsty. They walked quickly in the opposite direction to the noise. After about half an hour they could feel a light warm breeze and then the rotten fish smell of graks. Kenny stopped and pulled at Kirsty's arm.

"We've no choice. I think I can see light ahead," said Kirsty. She held onto the boy's hand and walked down the corridor towards the light.

When they got closer the light turned out to be a hazy mist. They walked into the swirling whiteness. Strange slurping and croaking noises from unseen creatures seemed to surround them. The mist cleared in patches and Kirsty could see for several metres in front of her. They were out of the tunnel and now walking on a soggy path through a swamp.

"This must be the Bog Lands," said Kirsty.

The Bog Lands

"Who goes there?" shouted Olaf.

Angus almost jumped out of his skin and pulled out his frostick. Wilfred turned to look at him. They had been walking in the mist for several hours. The weird landscape of the Bog Lands played on your mind. A patch of mist cleared and the moon shone down through giant bog cotton and gnarled bog roots.

"What are you up to?" asked Wilfred.

"I thought I saw someone in the distance. Near that stand of bog cotton. See over there! Near that dead tree. A man in a cloak I think," said Olaf. Angus peered through the mist. An old gnarled tree stood up out of the mist like a twisted claw.

"I see him!" said Angus. A man wearing dark robes was making his way through the marshes towards them. As he got closer Angus recognized him. The man stopped a few metres from them.

"What are you doing here Soyean?" asked Olaf.

Soyean bowed and said, "I assume that I am doing the same as you. I am looking for the new female Mind Caster,"

"My sister's name is Kirsty," said Angus.

"Oh yes Kirsty. Quite so, quite so," smiled Soyean.

"How did you get here?" asked Olaf.

"I took the trail from the northern nursery and over the mountains."

"Well, have you seen any trace of her?" asked Olaf.

"Well I did see something like a bit of cloth back that way. It's too far out in the bog to reach. I was looking for help when I bumped into you. Come I'll show you," smiled Soyean. He turned and walked back down the path he had come from. Angus didn't trust him and he was really worried that Kirsty had been sucked into the bog.

"Come on," said Wilfred.

They followed Soyean along the path as it wound around great black bogs. After several minutes Olaf called out," Are we going the right way. Where is this bog with the cloth in it?"

"Not far. We're nearly there," shouted Soyean. He made a high whistling noise. Suddenly there was a strong stench of rotting fish. Graks erupted from bogs on either sides of the path. One lashed out at Olaf but he pulled out his frostick and blasted it. It froze in midstrike.

"Angus!" shouted Wilfred as he pushed Angus out of the way. The creature came crashing down on Wilfred. Angus could see Wilfred's feet struggling as they stuck out from under the grak and hear his muffled screams. Angus struggled to his feet and tried to find his frostick. He saw it less than half a metre away. It was sinking into the bog. It must have fallen from his pocket. He stretched to reach for it but it sunk out of trace.

He turned to the grak smothering Wilfred and began beating at it with his bare hands. He remembered Kirsty's stone and got it out. He started to hit the grak with it. Another grak reared up out of the bog and slithered towards Angus. Olaf blasted it and it became a hideous frozen sculpture.

"Out of the way Angus!" shouted Olaf. "I'll blast it." Angus ducked out of the way and Olaf fired at the grak covering Wilfred. The creature's skin froze and split. Green gunge squirted out from the cracks. The smell was like ammonia.

"It's running out of freeze power," said Olaf.

The grak squirmed off Wilfred and dropped down into the bog. Angus looked down at Wilfred. He was covered in blood. His eyes were wide open and blank. Angus sat down beside him.

"Wilfred. Are you okay?" said Angus.

Another grak rose from the bog, Olaf blasted it. The grak's skin split, but only slightly. The creature let out a clicking noise. Olaf came up to Wilfred and felt for a pulse.

"He's still alive. He's in shock," said Olaf.

"Well how nice to bump into you. I must be going now," shouted Soyean from the other side of a bog.

"What. Help us man!" shouted Olaf.

"My clones are waiting for me. Destiny awaits," said Soyean.

"This man needs help or he will die," shouted Olaf.

"Yes that's the general idea. I'll leave my pets to finish you off," shouted Soyean.

"You traitor!" shouted Olaf. Soyean bowed and then walked off into the mist.

"Quick. Where's your frostick?" asked Olaf.

"When Wilfred saved me it got knocked into that bog," said Angus.

Olaf started looking through Wilfred's tattered and blood-soaked cloak.

"Wilfred's still got his one somewhere," said Olaf.

There were several clicking noises coming closer.

"We better find it quick. They're coming in for another attack," said Olaf.

Angus saw something glinting in the mud beside Wilfred's feet. He picked it up. It was the frostick. He gave it to Olaf. There was a noise like a motorbike revving up and a grak reared up out of the bog. Olaf blasted it. The grak made a loud clicking sound as it rolled around in the bog in agony. Another grak rushed at them. Olaf fired at it but missed by a few centimetres. He got it on the second blast. The grak slithered away.

The bog became silent.

"I think that's it for now. We've got to get out of this place before they attack again," said Olaf. He looked over Wilfred. He tore a piece of his cloak and tied it around Wilfred's right thigh. He pulled up a clump of sphagnum moss.

"What are you doing?" asked Angus.

"The moss contains a natural antiseptic," said Olaf. He lifted Wilfred up and draped him over his shoulder.

"Here. You take this. My hands are full," said Olaf. He handed the frostick to Angus.

"Which way will we go?" asked Angus.

"We can't go back the way. We wouldn't make it in the one boat. We'll have to go forward," said Olaf.

"I never liked that Soyean," said Angus, "I knew there was something bad about him."

"So he's the one behind the disappearances. He called the graks his pets. And what did he mean about his clones?" said Olaf.

"He must have Kirsty if he controls the graks. But he said he was looking for her too," said Angus.

"Well, let's go in the direction that he went in," said Olaf.

"There are so many little paths winding back and fore. I'm really not sure which way he went," said Angus. "I'll try my best. I think we go this way."

They made slow progress. Olaf had to carry Wilfred and also had to try and keep to the muddy path winding through a treacherous bog in the mist. Angus was on the look out for another surprise attack by graks. He held the frostick out in front of him. After they had been walking for an hour the mist cleared slightly. Angus saw a huge rock sticking up out of the mist, in the distance.

"There's a tor! Solid ground," said Angus.

"Okay head for it. It will be a safer place to rest. I 'm tired," said Olaf.

The tor had disappeared into the mist but Angus headed in its general direction. Angus guessed that he was about half way to the rock when he smelled sweetness on the mist. It was like the mist had been coated in honey. His stomach gurgled, reminding him that he hadn't eaten for ages.

"Olaf can you smell that? A sweet smell like honey?" said Angus. He yawned. "I feel really sleepy."

"Watch out. That's nectar. That means.." said Olaf. Before he could finish his sentence a massive hairy tentacle covered in sticky goo, ripped

Wilfred off Olaf's back. Wilfred was dragged off into the mist. Angus fired the frostick in its direction. Another sticky tentacle knocked the frostick from his hand then stuck itself to Angus's back. He was hauled into the air and pulled backward. He could see monstrous wriggling shadows in the mist all around him.

"Olaf!" shouted Angus. He heard Olaf shouting his name back and then Angus passed out.

When Angus awoke he couldn't move. His arms and legs were trapped. The tentacle had curved itself into a spoon shape. He was suspended three metres above the bog. The tentacle seemed to be one of many emerging from a huge plant. The sun was trying to break through the mist. Visibility was ten metres. He looked around and saw Wilfred was also wrapped in a tentacle.

"Angus!" shouted Olaf. Angus twisted his head around and saw Olaf suspended in another tentacle.

"You've been out for hours!" said Olaf.

"What's this!" said Angus.

"Giant sundew. Carnivorous plants," said Olaf.

"What a way to go. We'll be eaten alive, dissolved slowly," moaned Angus.

"Calm down! Let me think. Where's your frostick?" asked Olaf.

"It knocked it out of my hand. I can't see it anywhere," said Angus. He twisted his head round and scanned the ground. He said, "Anyway I can't move. Even if I saw it I wouldn't be able to get to it. This is getting really itchy. " Angus tried to struggle. The edges of the tentacle curled in slightly and sticky goo pumped up from the hairs.

"Yeuk!" said Angus.

"Don't move. Keep as still as possible. The plant pumps dissolving juices over you when you struggle," said Olaf.

"I feel like a fly caught on sticky paper," said Angus.

"Well, let's hope there's no spiders around," said Olaf.

"Or graks," replied Angus.

"Arrrgggg," moaned a voice.

Angus and Olaf looked around. It was Wilfred. He was stirring. The plant curled round him and sprayed him with dissolving juices.

"What are we going to do?" said Angus.

"Just let me think. Do you still have the stone?" asked Olaf.

"No I dropped it. But I can see it. It's below you on the path. That's strange," said Angus.

"What?" said Olaf.

"It's glowing. The stone is glowing," said Angus.

"That means that Kirsty must be near. Try shouting out to her," said Olaf.

"Kirsty! We're here!" shouted Angus.

"Kirsty. Watch out for the sundew!" shouted Olaf.

They kept on shouting for several minutes.

"Did you hear that?" said Angus. They both stopped and listened. In the distance they heard a faint noise. The noise got louder.

"Angus!"

"Kirsty!" shouted both Angus and Olaf.

"Angus!" came back the voice. Kirsty and a boy, looking much like Kallid appeared out of the mist.

"Kirsty you're okay!" said Angus.

"Don't come too close. Watch out for the sundew. It shoots a spray of nectar that makes you drowsy," said Olaf.

Kirsty stopped walking and said, "Are you injured Angus? Olaf?"

"Our friend Wilfred's lost a lot of blood. He's unconscious," said Angus.

The cloned boy grabbed Kirsty's hand. Kirsty turned round and looked at him.

"This is Kenny. He helped me to escape from Soyean's laboratory," said Kirsty.

"Hello Kenny," said Angus. He felt the image of a sun appear in his mind.

"Kenny talks with mind pictures," said Kirsty.

"I know. I just got one," said Angus.

"Right. We are going to get you out of this. Kenny is going to help me," said Kirsty.

Kirsty and Kenny held hands and stared at the scrying stone lying on the path below Olaf. The stone slowly floated up into the air and started to spin. It spun faster and faster until it was a whirling ball of fuzzy blue motion. They guided it towards the lower end of the tentacle holding Olaf and forced it to cut into the plant flesh. The plant shook violently. Olaf and Wilfred landed on the path but Angus fell into the bog. The stone came rushing up to Kirsty and she put it into a pocket in her cloak. The giant sundew curled itself up into a ball. Olaf stretched out on the path to grab Angus but he couldn't reach. He took off his cloak and threw one end to Angus. Angus managed to grab it on the second throw. He tried not to imagine the other creatures that could be lurking underneath him as he pulled himself across the bog. Olaf helped him out. Kirsty came up and gave Angus a hug.

"You're safe," said Kirsty. She also gave Olaf a hug. Olaf was a bit embarrassed and shrugged her off.

"I best tend to Wilfred," muttered Olaf. He went over to where Wilfred was lying out on the path. He looked very pale. Olaf tried to find a pulse. He put his ear to Wilfred's chest.

"He's dying. Wilfred's stopped breathing," said Olaf.

Kenny moved past Kirsty and came up to Olaf. He picked some up moss and wiped Wilfred's forehead. He laid a hand across Wilfred's forehead. He shut his eyes. Kenny's hand began to glow with a pale blue light. Wilfred stirred and opened his eyes.

"Olaf. Where are we? What happened? Kallid is that you?" said Wilfred. He tried to sit up but fell back.

"Woah! Don't try too fast. You've lost a lot of blood. You're lucky to be alive," said Olaf. Kenny got up and went back to stand beside Kirsty. Angus came over and helped Olaf to lift Wilfred up.

Kirsty came up to them and said, "Soyean is mad. He's planning something. We've got to get back to the Monastery and warn the Keeper."

"What is he up to?" asked Olaf.

"He's being doing secret cloning experiments. Kenny was cloned from Brother Gareth, "said Kirsty.

Olaf looked at Kenny and said, "But Brother Gareth only went missing three months ago. It would take years to grow a human clone to his age."

"It's possible. The Keeper told me about the mortality gene. It speeds up development but it's been banned for a long time," said Angus.

Kirsty said," Whatever kind of human Kenny is, he saved your friend's life and now it's drained him. We need to find somewhere safe to rest for a while."

Olaf said, "Yes we're all tired out. Where's that tor we saw before we were attacked by the sundew?"

"Kenny and I were climbing up it when we heard you shouting. It's not far. We're sitting ducks on this path. Come on. I'll show you the way," said Kirsty.

She walked along the path, followed by Kenny. Angus and Olaf helped Wilfred. They soon arrived at the tor. It jutted up out of the mist. Kirsty walked up a rough path that climbed up between rocks. After a minute she turned off the main path and walked out onto a wide stone ledge.

"This is as far as we got. We were resting here when we heard you shouting," said Kirsty.

"This will do fine for a rest," said Olaf. He and Angus laid Wilfred down.

"I'll take first watch," said Kirsty. Kenny came and sat down beside Kirsty. The others lay down and soon all them were sound asleep. Kenny touched Kirsty's hand. She looked at him. He looked older. His eyes were sunken and there were wrinkles starting to appear around his mouth and eyes.

"You look terrible. What's happening?" asked Kirsty. Kenny flashed images of the laboratory.

"You need to get back to the laboratory?" asked Kirsty. Kenny's eyes widened in fear. He forcefully shook his head.

"It's the mortality gene isn't it?" said Kirsty. Kenny nodded.

"It's happening even faster because you saved Wilfred?" said Kirsty. Kenny shrugged his shoulders. He flashed an image of the sun into her head.

"You want to watch the sun come up with me?" said Kirsty. Kenny nodded. Over the next hour they watched the night sky become lighter as the mist gradually fell away and waited for the dawn. Kirsty must have fallen asleep because when she woke up the sun was up.

"Look there's the sun. Isn't it beautiful!" said Kirsty. She turned to Kenny. He was laid out beside her; all dried up and light like an Egyptian mummy. He looked like he was smiling and his face was covered in wrinkles.

"Oh Kenny! I hope you got to see the dawn," sobbed Kirsty. She touched his arm. He fell apart into a cloud of dust. She stood up and looked out over the Bog Lands to the mountains making up the crater rim. To her right the Bog Lands petered out and became mud flats then a swirling blue sea.

Angus woke up. He got up and stood beside Kirsty.

"What happened to Kenny?" He looked at the empty labcoat lying on the rock.

"He's gone," said Kirsty. She sniffed. "Come on, let's climb this tor and see what's round the other side.

Angus and Kirsty walked up the steep slope. The path curved round up the rock and after a few minutes they came out to the summit of the tor. To the north mountains bordered the bog. They swept down to cliffs and at their base more mud flats. There was a stack at the end of the cliffs with a dark cloud hovering over it.

"The Stack of the Storm Hags!" said Kirsty.

"They'd know what to do," said Angus.

"Yes. They could send Birog and Crok to warn Lady Morgana and the Keeper," said Kirsty. "We should go now while the mist has cleared. I can't see any graks."

"We could cut right across the mud flats," said Angus.

Kirsty pointed out to sea and said, "No. The tide could come in really fast. Remember the Corriekraken Whirlpool."

Angus nodded, and said, "Let's get the others moving then." They walked back down the path.

"You wake them up. There's something I've got to do," said Kirsty. She picked up the labcoat and folded it up. She went back up the path to the summit of the tor. She gathered a small pile of stones and built a cairn.

When she got back down no one mentioned Kenny.

"Come on then!" said Kirsty.

They went back down the steep rocky path of the tor. Kirsty led, followed by Angus. Wilfred could now manage to walk by himself. Olaf walked behind him. In the sunshine the Bog Lands didn't look so forbidding. There were no strong smells of graks. Patches of giant bog cotton gleamed in the sun. Kirsty spotted a few sundew plants, well before they were within tentacle range, and managed to find a path around them.

An hour later they walked out of the Bog Lands and onto the mud flats. Everyone looked out to sea. They could see the swirling waters of the Corriekraken whirlpool.

"We'll keep to the edge of these mud flats. The tides are strong," said Olaf. He took the lead and started to walk around the shore. After a few minutes he saw something sticking up out of the sand. Kirsty ran past him and pulled the thing up out of the sand.

It was an old cork life belt painted with the letters "Marianne".

Angus came running up and looked at the life belt.

"Maybe they did get this far," said Angus. He looked out at the swirling whirlpool.

"I don't know," said Kirsty. She picked up the lifebelt and carried it over her shoulder.

They continued along the shore.

Storm Raft. © David Hutchison.

Psychic Shoog

Around the base of the stack it was snowing. The basket dangled from the rope. There was a big hole in the bottom of it. Olaf went up to it and gave the rope a yank. He looked up into the snow.

"Hello!" shouted Olaf. There was no reply. "I don't like this. They never leave the basket down. I'm going to have to climb up there."

"I should be the one to go up. I'm the best climber," said Wilfred.

"You're still weak. I will go," said Olaf.

"Nonsense. I feel better than I've ever been," said Wilfred. "When I get to the top I'll give the rope a jerk if it's safe to come up and I'll winch the basket up."

"That basket's no use. Here. Kirsty took the lifebelt off her shoulder and tied it to the rope with a couple of hitches.

Wilfred stood up on the lifebelt and climbed up the rope like a monkey, even though it was slippery with snow. Everyone watched as he disappeared up into the snowy clouds.

"He's certainly got a head for heights," said Kirsty.

"I could probably do that too now. I can abseil," said Angus. Kirsty laughed.

A few minutes later the rope jerked twice.

"Okay. It's safe to go up," said Olaf. He made to sit in the lifebelt but Kirsty got there first.

"I'm going. It's my life belt!" said Kirsty. She jumped into the life belt and it started to go up into the air.

"Send it back down for me then," shouted up Olaf. He wasn't very happy about it.

"Be careful Kirsty," shouted Angus.

Kirsty kept her head level with the stack and didn't look down. She felt much safer sitting in the life belt, rather than the fisherman's basket but she still had a fear of heights. She looked up into the falling snow and made out Wilfred at the davit.

Soon she was on top of the stack. Wilfred swung the mechanical arm around and Kirsty's feet touched the rocky surface.

"I thought Olaf was coming up, not you!" said Wilfred. Kirsty shrugged her shoulders.

"Watch out. It's slippery," said Wilfred. He helped Kirsty to get out of the lifebelt.

"There's a Storm Hag sticking out of the snow in that hovel. I think she's dead. Can't find anyone else," said Wilfred.

Kirsty went to the shack. The tarpaulin had been torn off the doorway. Tattered rags flapped in the wind. Inside there were drifts of snow piled up against the walls. Shelves had been pulled down. Parts of the roof had been hauled down. There was a lump lying on the floor against a fish box. A blue arm poked out of a drift of snow piled up against the stove. Kirsty rushed up to the pile and cleared the snow with her hands. It was Halibutina huddled up in her seaweed cloak. Bits of ice had fused parts of the seaweed together. She was shivering.

Kirsty said, "Halibutina. Are you okay?"

"Och Kirsty! Git the fire gaun an a'll be fine. Gat antifreeze in ma bluid!" said Halibutina.

"Can you get a fire on?" said Kirsty to Wilfred. He nodded and began to clean snow off the stove. He gathered some sticks and started to make a fire as Kirsty dug Halibutina out of the snowdrift.

"What happened here?" asked Kirsty.

"It wis Soyean. I thocht ye war wi him sae it wis awricht tae bring to yese up. A'm a bawheid.."

"What's a bawheid?" said Kirsty.

"A bawheid? An eediot. She wis a clone. A shoud hae kent whan she wadnae speak tae me. I hoised thaim up in the creel an brocht thaim intae the hoose. Thay stealt the Brahan stane. A tried tae fecht but he wis ower pouerfu," said Halibutina.

"Soyean. We were coming here to warn you. He's gone totally mad. He's being doing his own cloning experiments. He's got control over the graks too," said Kirsty.

Wilfred had got the fire lit. He pulled a fish box in front of it. Kirsty helped Halibutina to sit on the fish box in front of the stove.

"Where's Nellbridy and Kerigayle?" said Kirsty.

"Thay gaed tae the Monastery whan thay kent ye haed been wheeched awa. A bade here tae leuk ower the stane. Ye maun git it. T'will mak him ower pouerfu," said Halibutina.

"How are you feeling now?" asked Kirsty.

"Wairm saut bree's whit a need," said Halibutina. "Thare's a lippin-fou bowie unner the table."

Wilfred got out the bucket and poured the seawater into a large pot on the stove.

The ravens Birog and Crok flew into the room. They landed in Halibutina's lap and made crowing and screeching noises. Her eyes widened and she gasped.

"Unco news! The Keeper haes been kilt!" said Halibutina.

"What? The Keeper dead?" said Wilfred.

99

"Ma sisters?" said Halibutina to the ravens. Birog made screeching noises. Crok got up and flew in circles above her head.

"What did they say?" asked Wilfred.

"An unco strang wappon at the Temple o Suil an blew hauf the Monastery awa." said Halibutina. "Thay're trying tae attack this wappon. Thay need help. A'll rousle up a storm raft tae tak us thare."

Birog and Crok squawked again. Halibutina nodded. "Ay, gae an tell thaim we are on oor wey!" The ravens flew out of the shack.

"That watter maun be wairm!" said Halibutina. She picked it up and poured it over her head." She stretched and said, "A feel better. Gaither up twa-three nets intae a muckle bing thareoot."

Wilfred and Kirsty went out of the shack. Sticking up out of the snow were different coloured piles of net amongst plastic and wooden fish boxes.

"We need tae git twa-three bings an tie thaim thegither tae mak a muckle cushin," said Halbutina. She moved fish boxes out of the way and created a large cleared area.

"I'll get help," said Wilfred. He went to the davit and let the rope and lifebelt down. A few minutes later he hauled up Angus and Olaf. They were squashed together holding onto the lifebelt. Wilfred swung them round on the mechanical arm and then onto the stack's summit.

"What took you so long!" said Olaf

"The Keeper is dead," said Wilfred.

"Dead?" said Olaf.

"The Keeper. How?"asked Angus.

"Soyean blasted the Monastery," said Kirsty.

"What with? How?" said Olaf.

"He's stolen the Brahan stone and is using it as a weapon. Nellbridy and Kerigayle are fighting him right now. We must go and help them," said Kirsty.

"He got here before us. He tricked Halibutina with a clone of Kirsty." said Wilfred.

"The storm raft is ready. Awbody git on nou," said Halibutina. She was standing on top of the pile of nets. "A'v makkit twa-three raips for haudles."

The pile of nets was around three metres across. Everyone jammed together and held tightly onto the ropes. Halibutina held her hands in the air and began to twist them as if she was winding a ball of invisible wool in the air above her. There was a cold wind that started to spin around then. The wind pulled up the fallen snow. A funnel of white swirling snow moved faster and faster around the storm raft. The storm tightened and narrowed until it became a mini-cyclone. The raft began to rise in the howling wind.

"Up an awa!" cried out Halibutina.

They soared up into the wind and away from the stack. Patches of living blue sand spread away in all directions as the cyclone passed over the Dark Shore. The cyclone gathered up sand and light black pebbles. Everyone had to spit out the sand and cover his or her face, except Halibutina, who seemed to enjoy it. She flew them over the cliffs and towards Mount Suil. They could see the valley with the village getting nearer when suddenly a bright blue light hit the cyclone. The raft was flung to the south. Halibutina was knocked down. Kirsty grabbed hold of her. The cyclone vanished and the storm raft started to fall from the sky.

"Halibutina! Wake up!" shouted Kirsty.

"We're going too fast. We'll crash," shouted Angus.

"Kirsty try your stone!" shouted Angus. Kirsty tried to get her stone from her pocket in her cloak. Suddenly the raft swerved south. It fell towards the Caldera Gardens and landed in a muddy field of giant leeks.

"Phew. That was close. Thanks Kirsty!" said Angus. He stood up and looked around. No one was hurt. Halibutina was still unconscious.

"It wasn't me. Where are we?" said Kirsty.

"The Caldera Gardens," said Olaf.

Lady Morgana came running down the path. She was pretty fast for an old lady. She had a makeshift bandage wrapped around her head.

"Are you all okay?"gasped Lady Morgana. "I only just managed to divert you from crashing into the sea. "

"It was you. Thanks!" said Angus.

"Is Halibutina okay?" asked Lady Morgana.

"I don't know. She's still breathing. She was struck by the blue fire," said Kirsty.

"Where are Nellbridy and Kerigayle?" asked Olaf.

Lady Morgana wrung her hands and said, "I'll tell you about them later. Quick we must get under cover before there is another blast. Follow me!"

Lady Morgana ran along the path and the others followed her as she made for the Mendelian Temple.

"We'll be an easy target in there," shouted Olaf. Lady Morgana ran up the steps and opened the doors of the temple. She went into the middle of the room and crouched down on the floor.

"Oh, where is it? Where is it now?" she muttered.

"What are you doing?" asked Kirsty.

There was a blinding flash of light and the whole temple shook.

Angus ran to the temple door, looked out and shouted, "That was the storm raft. It's been blown up."

Ah, there you are!" muttered Lady Morgana. She pressed an apple shape carved into the marble floor. There was a noise of gears moving and part of the marble floor slid away to reveal a staircase. Lady Morgana took a glow globe from her blue cloak and descended the stairs. She said, "Everyone come on."

"I never even knew that this was here," said Olaf, as he and Wilfred carried Halibutina down the steps.

"It's a secret way into the Monastery," said Lady Morgana. "Nellbridy showed it to me many years ago, when I was a child."

The marble floor slid back into place behind them. This tunnel was much smaller than the usual tunnels burrowed into the Monastery. It was crudely hewn and smelled damp. Olaf still had a glow globe so he gave it to Kirsty to hold. After about fifteen minutes of walking the tunnel opened out into a large hall with several doors going off it. In the middle of the hall was a well. It had thick wide stone edges, an iron structure with a handle, and wooden bucket tied to a rope. Lady Morgana went and sat on the edge of the well. Olaf and Wilfred propped Halibutina up against the side of the well.

"We're under the mountain. I think we're safe for now," said Lady Morgana.

As if on cue there was a tremendous noise and a shockwave rippled through the hall. Small bits the roof showered down on them, covering them in dust

"How did the Keeper die?" asked Olaf.

"When I heard that Kirsty had been kidnapped I tried to look into my scrying stone to see if I could find her. At first it was the usual mist then I had a vision. Kirsty split up into many Kirstys and they formed a circle. Wild blue fire streamed from their eyes and I saw the Eye Tower explode. Then I saw Soyean. His face was distorted in rage. I was really confused," said Lady Morgana.

"He's gone mad. He kidnapped me and took my blood to make clones with," said Kirsty.

"I thought he'd been acting strangely! How could a Mind Caster have access to the cloning technology? " asked Lady Morgana.

"He said that he got his knowledge from research sites on the Internet," said Kirsty.

"The Internet?" asked Lady Morgana.

"It's a network of computers linked together around the world. I suppose he must have linked into it via his scrying stone," said Angus.

"I understand. Anyway I looked around the village for Soyean. I wanted to confront him but I couldn't find him anywhere. All the Mind Casters were walking around as if in a trance. I spoke to Kallid. He just stared at me as if I wasn't there. I got out of that village quickly. I sent word to the Storm Hags to meet me at the Monastery as I also wanted to speak with the Keeper," said Lady Morgana.

Kirsty said, "Soyean used a clone of me to trick Halibutina into letting him up the stack. He stole the Brahan stone from her."

Lady Morgana said, "I was in the Grand Hall with the Keeper, Nellbridy and Kerigayle. We were figuring out who was behind Kirsty's kidnapping. I was telling them about my fellow Mind Casters going strange and my suspicions about Soyean when suddenly there was a splitting blue flash and the window shattered. We were thrown from our feet and I lost consciousness. When I woke up I had blood bleeding down my head and into my eyes. The Keeper lay out on the floor near me. He had been ripped to shreds by splinters of glass and was dying. His last words to me were that you are to take over from him Olaf."

"What me?" asked Olaf.

"Yes. You are the Keeper now," said Lady Morgana. Halibutina stirred. She opened her eyes.

"Whaur am a? Whit happent?" said Halibutina.

"We're in an underground chamber. You're safe for the moment. We were blasted out of the sky. Lady Morgana saved us," said Kirsty.

"A mynd nou. The blast. Whit aboot ma sisters?" asked Halibutina.

"As I was saying a blast of blue light hit the Grand Hall and shattered the window, killing the Keeper. Luckily a pillar had sheltered your sisters and me from most of the flying glass. Your sisters got on their storm raft and brewed up a cyclone. I watched them fly up into the sky, heading for Mount Suil.

"Guid on thaim!" said Halbutina.

As they were flying up out of the Gardens a bolt of blue fire blasted them out of the sky. I saw them fall into the orchard. I tried to break their fall but I was still too weak from the blast. I organised the Sowers to take shelter in the deeper tunnels. Then I went to the gardens to find Nellbridy and Kerigayle, when you appeared in the sky. Luckily I had recovered enough to help you land."

"A maum ken whit's happent tae ma sisters," said Halibuntina. She tried to stand up but fell down.

"Stay here. You are too weak. One of us will go," said Olaf.

Halibutina said, "Whan yese git oot cry Birog and Crok. Thay'll lead yese tae ma sisters."

Olaf and Wilfred got up.

"I'm coming too," said Angus.

"Okay. Kirsty will you and Lady Morgana look after Halibutina?" said Olaf. Kirsty nodded.

Lady Morgana said," Don't go back the same way. Take that door over there." She pointed to a wooden door at one end of the hall. "Go through there and along the tunnel to the left for a hundred metres. You will come to a set of steps leading upwards. Follow them and you will come to a cave mouth covered in bushes. Go through the bushes and you will be in the orchard."

"Along the left tunnel, up steps, out of the cave into the orchard," said Olaf. Lady Morgana nodded.

"Be careful," said Kirsty.

Angus, Olaf and Wilfred went off out the door. As Lady Morgana had said, they found the steps after about a hundred metres. They climbed them and came to the cave mouth.

"Wait here a sec," said Olaf. He disappeared through the bushes at the cave mouth. He came back shortly and said, "All clear. There's about a twenty metre stretch of bare grass before we're covered by the orchard so get ready to run when I say so." Angus and Wilfred nodded. Olaf pushed through the bushes, followed by Angus then Wilfred. They crowded together at the outer edge of the bush.

"Look up there," said Angus. He pointed up into the sky. Two black dots were circling high above. "It's Birog and Crok."

Wilfred said, "They're flying over the north end of the orchard. That's where the Storm Hags must be."

Olaf said, "Are you ready to run for that apple tree?"

"Yes," said Angus and Wilfred together.

"Now!" said Olaf.

They ran out of the bush and across the grass the orchard, each expecting to be blasted with blue flames at any second. They reached the cover of the golden apple tree without any incident.

"Birog, Crok!" shouted Olaf.

"Birog!" shouted Angus.

"Crok!" shouted Wilfred.

There was a screeching noise and the ravens flew down to them. Birog landed on Angus's shoulder and Crok flew around their heads. Crok flew off to a tree further away. Birog got up and flew onto a branch above her.

"Follow them. They're leading the way," said Wilfred.

They followed the ravens through the orchard until they got to the north side where they found an area of broken branches and piles of nets. Nellbridy and Kerigayle were lying together on some orange plastic nets. Birog and Crok flew down beside them. Olaf knelt down to examine the Storm Hags. Their skin had changed from a normal dark blue to a pale purple.

"Are they dead?" asked Angus.

"They're not breathing. Their bodies are frozen like ice," said Olaf.

Wilfred bent down and looked at Kerigayle. Her red hair had turned pink. One of her eyes blinked.

"She's alive!" said Wilfred. "I saw her blink." He held Kerigayle's hand and rubbed it.

"Nellbridy did too," said Olaf. "They seem to be in some kind of shock. Can move their eyelids but nothing else. We'll have to carry them back.

"How are we going to do that?" asked Angus. He looked at the bulky Kerigayle.

Olaf unraveled one of the piles of nets. He laid it out on the grass and folded it until it was like a thin mattress.

"We'll use the net as a sled to drag them. Help me get Kerigayle onto this," said Olaf.

Wilfred and Angus grabbed Kerigayle's legs. Olaf held her arms. They carried her onto the net.

"Now Nellbridy," said Olaf. She was much lighter and was easily moved. Olaf looked around and found some bits of rope. He tied three bits to one end of the net.

"Let's try it," said Olaf.

Olaf, Angus and Wilfred positioned themselves at the head of the net and took the strain of the ropes.

"One, two, three, heave!" shouted Olaf.

They heaved and the net started moving.

"Keep the momentum up," said Wilfred. They dragged the net through the orchard. Birog and Crok flew from tree to tree, squawking away as if giving encouragement. It was heavy going but in half an hour they were back at the apple tree beside the grassy patch. Olaf checked the Storm Hags but there was no change. They rested for a few minutes then got to their feet. Birog and Crok flew onto the bush hiding the cave mouth.

"Now this is going to be the most dangerous bit," said Olaf. "Are we ready?"

"Yes," said Angus.

"Yes," said Wilfred.

"Three, two, one, go!" said Olaf. They moved as fast as possible, dragging the net with the Storm Hags towards the hidden cave mouth. Just when they had got a few metres left to go, Nellbridy rolled off the net.

"I'll get her!" said Wilfred. "You get Kerigayle into cover!"

There wasn't time to argue so Olaf and Angus dragged the net as quickly into the bushes as they could. There was a blinding flash and Wilfred screamed in agony. Angus turned round to see Wilfred go flying up in the air and land beside the bush. He was dead. His neck was broken.

"Wilfred!" screamed Angus. He stood shivering with fright as Olaf jumped out of the bush and dragged Nellbridy under cover.

"Go, go!" shouted Olaf. They wrapped the net around Kerigayle and dragged her through the bushes into the tunnel. They went back and carried Nellbridy into the tunnel.

Another bolt of blue flames struck. It burnt the bush to a cinder.

"Go and get Kirsty and Lady Morgana to help us," coughed Olaf. Angus ran along the tunnel, down the steps, three at a time and along the corridor.

"Quick, Kirsty, Lady Morgana, we need help!" shouted Angus.

Kirsty and Lady Morgana got up and ran to the door,

"Are thay bemangit?" shouted Halibutina as they ran out the door. Angus didn't answer. Olaf had dragged the Storm Hags to the top of the steps. The tunnel behind him was full of smoke. Angus and Olaf carried Kerigayle, wrapped in the net, down the steps and along the corridor to the hall. Lady Morgana and Kirsty followed with the lighter Nellbridy, but it was too much for Lady Morgana. Angus and Olaf laid the Storm Hags down on the ground on either side of Halibutina. Olaf went back and took over from Lady Morgana. Halibutina felt Nellbridy's and then Kerigayle's foreheads.

"Psychic shoog, peelie-wallie. Thay'll dee gin thay dinnae git the remeed gin day-set," said Halibutina.

"What's the remedy?" asked Lady Morgana.

"Scales frae a daimen fish. It bides in the Loch of the Gowden Carp," said Halibutina.

"Don't you mean the Loch of the Golden Harp?" said Olaf.

"No, Loch of the Gowden Carp," said Halibutina.

"Wilfred said it was..anyway I think I know where it is," said Olaf.

"Where is Wilfred?" asked Kirsty.

"He didn't make it," said Olaf.

"Oh no!" said Kirsty.

Angus was sitting on the edge of the well looking down into the water. Kirsty went up to him and put her arm on his shoulder. She could see tears streaking down his face.

"Are you okay?" said Kirsty.

"Course I'm not okay!" stammered Angus. "Wilfred saved my life in the caves. He saved Nellbridy too. I thought he was invincible and now he's dead. I want to kill that Soyean!"

Olaf came over and sat beside Angus. "I feel really awful too Angus but we haven't time to grieve. If Wilfred's sacrifice is to mean anything we have to keep going."

"I know that," sniffed Angus.

"The Storm Hags still need our help. We have to go back to that underground loch," said Olaf.

"Why?" asked Angus.

"Because there is a rare fish that lives in it and we need to bring some of its scales back to cure Nellbridy and Kerigayle," said Olaf.

"What kind of fish?" asked Angus.

"A golden carp," said Olaf.

"Wilfred called it *The Loch of the Golden Harp*. That's funny," said Angus. "He never finished telling me the story of the magic golden harp. Do you know it?" asked Angus.

"No, sorry," said Olaf. He patted Angus on the back. "Try and rest for a while. We'll leave in an hour."

"I don't suppose any of you have eaten? I'll go and find us some food. Kirsty will you come and help me?" said Lady Morgana.

"Sure," said Kirsty. She followed Lady Morgana through the door and out of the room. This time they took a tunnel on the right side, which sloped upwards. They walked along it for fifteen minutes and then stopped at a wooden door. Lady Morgana pushed it open and entered a large room. There was a pleasant yeast and flour smell in the air. The far side had a window looking down to the Caldera Gardens. To the left were several massive ovens with pipes leading off them into a wide chimney. In the centre of the room was a long bleached wooden table. Shelves filled the right wall. They were stacked with large pottery jars.

"This is the Monastery bakery. We should find something here," said Lady Morgana. She went to the table and lifted the lid of the first jar.

"Ah, oatcakes. We'll have those. Kirsty get a basket. There should be one under the table somewhere," said Lady Morgana.

Kirsty found several baskets under the table on a low bench. She picked up a good sturdy wicker one. She found a small knife in a drawer and added it to the basket. Lady Morgana had opened more pottery jars and had found several loaves of bread and some wee currant cake slices that looked like fly cemetery. Kirsty put the oatcakes and then the bread into the basket. Lady Morgana opened a small pantry cupboard and found a jar of blunge jam and a large piece of goat's cheese wrapped up in a cloth. She put them in the basket.

"What about something to drink?" asked Kirsty.

"The water in the well's fine. We'll bring back a few cups," said Lady Morgana. She looked around and saw metal tumblers on a shelf. "Those up there. Can you get them? They're too high for me to reach."

Kirsty reached up and brought down some tumblers.

"Okay, that's enough. Let's get back," said Lady Morgana.

They left the bakery and went back down the tunnel. Soon they got back the hall. Kirsty sat down beside the well and cut the loaves up. She made blunge jam pieces and cut thick slices of goat's cheese for everyone.

"Keep ane bannock. The Gowden Carp hae a greenin for breid," said Halibutina.

Olaf turned the handle and lowered the bucket into the well. He brought it back up full and passed tumblers of sweet and fizzy water around.

Soon everyone had eaten his or her fill.

"We better get started then," said Kirsty.

"Only Angus and me are going. You can look after Lady Morgana and the Storm Hags," said Olaf.

"I don't need looking after and less of the orders. You're not the new keeper yet!" said Lady Morgana. Olaf blushed.

"I'm coming and that's final!" said Kirsty.

Olaf shrugged his shoulders and said, "Okay then. First we'd better go to the armoury and get some frosticks,"

"The blast has blocked the tunnel to the armoury. I'll get a team of Sowers to dig it out but it'll take several days," said Lady Morgana.

"We've got 'til sunset so we'll just have to improvise," said Olaf

"I've got a sharp knife," said Kirsty. "I don't like knives. You can have it Olaf." She handed the knife to him.

Lady Morgana took out a glow globe from a fold in her blue cloak and said, "I've still got some charge in this glow globe. Here, you take it Kirsty!"

"We'll need something to catch this golden carp. Any ideas Halibutina?" said Olaf.

"Mmmh. A snuid? Mynd yese anerly tak twa scales. Gin yese kilt it yese'll bring deem on us aw," said Halibutina.

"I'll remember,"said Olaf.

"There's the net under Kerigayle," said Kirsty.

"Of course," said Angus.

"Help me to roll her over," said Kirsty. She and Angus rolled Kerigayle over and pulled out the net. They rolled the net up into a tight bundle and put it in the wicker basket along with the spare loaf of bread.

"Right which way to the bedrooms off the Grand Hall? I forgot to ask. Did they get blown up too?" asked Olaf.

"That part of the Grand Hall is still intact and we've not moved the ropes. Do you know your way there from the bakery?" asked Lady Morgana. Olaf nodded.

"Well then Kirsty can show you how to get to the bakery," said Lady Morgana.

"Okay. Let's be off," said Olaf

"Good luck," said Lady Morgana. She gave Kirsty and Angus each a hug. Olaf stayed well back.

"Guid luck," said Halibutina and grabbed Kirsty's hand.

Kirsty led the way out of the hall. They took the right tunnel and after fifteen minutes Kirsty stopped at the door of the kitchen.

"The kitchen's in there," said Kirsty.

"I know where we are now," said Olaf. "We carry along this tunnel and then there's a flight of steps that go up through all the levels to the Grand Hall," He walked along the tunnel and in a little while they came across a wide stone staircase. They climbed up to the next level and came to a wide landing with several exits going off it. They carried on upwards. Each level looked the same as the previous one. When they reached the seventh level Olaf went down one of the tunnels. After several minutes they found themselves in what was left of the Hall of Tree Ferns. The huge glass window was shattered and burnt stumps of tree ferns lay scattered all around.

Kirsty sighed, "What a shame. It was such a beautiful room."

They left the hall and went down the tunnel. The door to the Grand Hall was lying open. The floor was covered in shards of glass and melted bubbles of lead. A fragment of the stained glass window still stuck to the window frame by a piece of twisted lead. It was the part with the two birds flying in the sky.

Kirsty pointed to the birds and said, "I think that's a good omen."

The tables and chairs were strewn around in bits and pieces. Olaf, Kirsty and Angus picked their way through the debris. No one mentioned the wide patch of dried blood in the middle of the room but they all knew that must have been where the Keeper died.

The ropes tied to the metal bed were still dangling out of Kirsty's bedroom.

Kirsty looked out of the window.

"I'm glad that I fainted when the graks took me down that cliff," said Kirsty.

Luckily there were plenty of extra harnesses lying on the floor. Angus showed Kirsty how to put them on, then put his one on.

"I'll go first, then Kirsty. Angus you come down last," said Olaf.

Olaf clipped the rope through his hook and got up onto the window ledge. He took the slack off the rope and climbed out with his back to the sea.

He started to walk down the side of the cliff.

"Right Kirsty. Start coming down now," Angus shouted up from below.

Kirsty was terrified but she gritted her teeth and stood up on the window ledge.

"Wait," shouted Angus.

"What?" asked Kirsty.

"You've forgotten to clip the rope through the hook," said Angus. He pulled the rope through the hook for her.

"Okay, down you go. Oh and watch out for nesting birds. One might fly out and scare you," said Angus.

Kirsty took the slack of the rope and leaned out of the window. She didn't dare look down but she could hear the waves crashing against the rocks way down below.

She stepped down with one foot, let out a bit of rope and then took another step. She studied the cliff face as she went down. It kept her mind off the drop below. She looked at the pattern the yellow lichen made on the rocks. She didn't come across any nesting birds but once a green lizard peeked at her from a crack. Soon she was two thirds of the way down the cliff. Kirsty looked up. Angus was a few metres above her.

Olaf shouted up to her, "You're doing fine."

She looked down. Olaf was standing on a ledge sticking out from the entrance to the cave. Her head started to spin. The rocks below seemed to be pulling her down, begging for her to jump to them.

"Kirsty are you okay!" shouted Angus. He had abseiled down to beside her.

"I'll be okay in a minute. I shouldn't have looked down," said Kirsty. Angus waited until Kirsty felt better and they went down the last third of the cliff together. Olaf pulled on their ropes. They swung into the cave and landed on the slippery seaweed floor.

Olaf shouted over the crashing waves, "Well done Kirsty."

Kirsty smiled as she took off her harness. Angus looked around the cave and shouted, "That's good. I can't smell any graks."

"Okay. I'll go first," shouted Olaf.

"You'd better take this then," shouted Kirsty. She got the glow globe out of her cloak and handed it to Olaf. He twisted it and went to the dark opening at the back of the cave. Kirsty and Angus followed him. After several minutes they came to the place where the tunnel split in two. Olaf stopped.

"We found your scrying stone up that tunnel on the left," said Angus.

"Yes, I remember dropping it," said Kirsty.

Olaf hurried along the left tunnel. After a short while the tunnel began to give off a green glow and Olaf shut off his glow globe.

"Luminous algae," said Angus to Kirsty.

"Do you remember any of this?" asked Olaf.

"Not much. It's like a nightmare. I only remember flashes of it. I was tied to the back of a grak. The smell was horrible. There was a herd of them and they made a chorus of clicking noises as we rushed through the tunnels. Soyean was shouting out commands," said Kirsty.

They walked in silence for the next half an hour. The tunnel eventually opened up into the huge cavern. They stood on the bank as the river flowed past them into the enormous cavern.

"The Loch of the Golden Carp," said Olaf.

"It looks very peaceful," said Kirsty. She looked down past the river mouth towards the expanse of still water. The luminous green of the high roof of the cavern was reflected in the water. Here and there stalactites and pillars formed secluded bays like alcoves in a cathedral.

"How did you cross the lake," asked Angus

"I was out for the count, most of the time. I don't really remember. The graks probably swam across it, " said Kirsty.

"We found a wee jetty up the river," said Angus, "But we lost one of the boats. The other's away at the other end of the lake."

They walked along the river to its mouth, where it fed into the lake. They sat down on the shore and looked across the dark expanse of water.

"So how are we going to catch this Golden Carp?" asked Kirsty.

"I wish I had a fishing rod, a hook and worm. Then I'd catch it easily," said Angus.

"I thought that we could lure it to the bank with some bread and then throw the net over it," said Olaf

Kirsty looked out across the massive loch and said, "We have to let it know there's bread for it. Throwing it in and hoping for the best won't do,"

"Also we need to find a place to use the net. A small bay that we can pull the net across to trap the Golden Carp when it comes for the bread," said Angus.

"We'll need to weigh one side of the net down so the fish doesn't slip under it," said Kirsty.

"Good idea. Angus you and Kirsty look for large pebbles to use as weights. I'll have a look around to see if I can find a small bay," said Olaf.

"Hadn't we better measure the net first to see what size of bay we are looking for?" said Kirsty.

Angus untied the net. Olaf helped him to stretch it out on the shore. Olaf walked along it.

"...thirty-nine, forty, forty-one. Forty-one footsteps. That's' about thirteen metres," said Olaf. "Right I'll go and look for a small bay less than thirteen metres"

Olaf headed off. Angus and Kirsty gather a pile of large pebbles. Angus sat down and unravelled the rope that had been used to tie the net into a bundle.

"What are you doing?" asked Kirsty.

"We can fold the bottom of the net over these pebbles and then hitch each pebble in. This rope's made of three strands, each four metres long, so if I unravel it we'll have twelve metres of rope," said Angus.

"Good idea. I'll space the pebbles out," said Kirsty.

111

An hour passed and they had finished weighing the net down. There was no sign of Olaf.

"He's been an awful long time. Do you think we should go and look for him?" asked Angus.

"Yes. I don't like sitting down here doing nothing. Help me roll the net up," said Kirsty.

They rolled the net up and put it into the wicker basket. Angus tried to lift it.

"Phew! I hope we've not made it too heavy. We should really have floats on the top of it," said Angus.

"It'll have to do," said Kirsty. She picked up the bread and put it on top of the net.

"Hello!" echoed a voice.

Kirsty and Angus looked down the shore and saw Olaf coming from behind a pile of boulders.

"Olaf, we were just coming to look for you," said Angus.

Olaf came up to them and said, "It took ages to find the right place. It's about a kilometre away." He picked up the basket. "Wow, you've certainly weighed it down."

"Do you think it's too heavy?" asked Angus.

"Can't really tell until we test it," said Olaf. "Let's get going."

Olaf walked back down the shore with Kirsty and Angus following behind. It was fairly easy going for most of the way. Kirsty and Angus carried the basket between them a few times to give Olaf a rest. They eventually came to a rocky outcrop and climbed over it to the other side. There was a bay on the other side.

"Is this the place?" asked Kirsty.

"No, too wide. There's a better place over the next ridge," said Olaf.

They walked across the shore and up over the ridge. On the top they looked down.

Below them was a small bay with a narrow inlet.

"Perfect!" said Angus.

They climbed down the rocks and stood on the shore of the small bay.

"Spread the net out on the beach," said Olaf. He untied a long rope that he had around his waist as Kirsty and Angus unfurled the net. Olaf got the knife out and cut his rope in half. He tied one end to the left topside of the net and the other to the top right side of the net.

"I'll grab this rope on the right and one of you take the left one. We're going walk along each side of the bay out to the points. Then we'll let out the rope so the net is lying along the bottom of the entrance to the bay," said Olaf.

"I'll do it. I'm bigger than Angus," said Kirsty.

"Not by much," said Angus. "I'm stronger."

"How about this then. You take the left side and help Olaf to get the net in position. I'll spread out the breadcrumbs and then come and help you," said Kirsty.

"Deal," said Angus.

"One other thing. Fish get scared off by noise so let's keep quiet until the Golden Carp is in the bay eating the bread," said Olaf.

"What do we do then?" said Kirsty.

"We pull the ropes up to block the bay. Then we slowly walk from the points back to the shore, dragging the net across the bay," said Olaf.

"Right you are skipper," said Angus.

"What?" asked Olaf.

"Nevermind. Come on let's catch the Golden Carp!" said Angus. He went to the left side of the net and held the rope. Olaf walked up to the right side and picked up the rope. They both began walking out to the points on either side of the small bay. When the top of the net was taught across the bay they let the ropes down and the net sank beneath the dark surface. Kirsty broke small pieces of bread off the loaf. She rubbed each one between her fingers until they looked like dough worms. When she had around a dozen worms she threw them out into the bay. The plopping noise echoed across the lake. Kirsty put the rest of the loaf into the basket and silently crossed the shore. She climbed the rock and walked along to the point. She sat down beside Angus and started to roll out some more dough worms.

After several minutes of total quiet Kirsty threw another dozen worms into the bay. There was the usual plopping noise and the echo. But there was another sound. A slight swishing noise, then it was gone. Angus peered out across the lake. About twenty metres out where the lake was reflecting the green cavern roof there was a ripple. There was another ripple and Angus saw a flash of gold under the water. He nudged Kirsty and pointed. She looked and saw the ripples moving towards the bay. Olaf waved to show that he had seen it too. Kirsty quickly broke of another piece of bread and made a dough worm. She threw it into the middle of the bay. They all strained their eyes to see into the water. There was just enough bread left to make another dough worm. Kirsty quickly made one and threw it into the bay.

About a metre before the dough worm hit the water the surface broke and a gigantic gold fish broke the surface and launched itself into the air. It snapped the dough worm into its mouth and splashed back down with slapping noise.

"Now!" shouted Olaf. He started pulling the rope up. Angus did the same. When the rope was tight and the net lay across the bay Olaf shouted, "Right, drag it slowly towards the shore,"

Angus held the net tight as he walked towards the shore. Suddenly the net jerked. Angus was dragged off his feet and Kirsty was knocked over. Angus tried to hold onto the rope but it raced through his hands and out into the lake.

"Hold it!" shouted Olaf.

"Arrgh," shouted Angus.

Olaf was still holding his end of the rope. It was jerking.

"Come and help me hold it. I think it's got tangled in the net," shouted Olaf. Kirsty ran down the rocks and around the bay. When she got up to the point Olaf was standing there with a slack net.

"It got away," he said.

"It almost worked, "said Kirsty.

"Yes but we don't have any bread now," said Olaf. He sat down. Angus walked round the bay and sat down beside Olaf.

"Sorry," said Angus.

"It's okay. I should have told you to hitch the rope around something," said Olaf.

"What are we going to do now," said Angus.

"At least we know that the bread works but now we don't have any left." said Kirsty.

"If I only had a fishing rod. I could catch it easily with a spinner," groaned Angus.

"What did you say Angus?" said Kirsty.

"If I only had a fishing rod. I could.." said Angus.

"Easily catch it with a spinner," finished Kirsty. She jumped up and took her scrying stone out of her cloak. "Your spinner."

They pulled the net ashore. Glistening in it was one large golden scale, the size of a saucer. Kirsty laughed and picked it up.

"Look. We only need one more."

They untangled the net and set up their positions on either side of the point again. Angus and Olaf had made sure that they had the rope doubled around an arm. Kirsty stood on the point beside Angus. The Loch of the Golden Carp was still. Kirsty took out her scrying stone. She thought of herself as a bird and the stone floated up into the air. She guided it over the loch. At about twenty metres out she let it spin, hovering above the surface. She thought of what would happen if the giant fish swallowed her scrying stone. She didn't think that she had enough telekinetic power to land the fish.

After a minute she saw a ripple of movement. Kirsty slowly brought the spinning stone towards the bay. The ripples followed. Kirsty moved the stone into the middle of the bay. It hovered a metre above the surface. There was a flash of gold and then the Golden Carp leaped out of the water. Kirsty barely managed to the move the stone in time.

114

"Now!" shouted Olaf. He pulled up his rope. Angus did the same.

Kirsty brought the scrying stone back to her hand and placed it into her cloak.

"Walk slowly to the beach. Keep a good grip on that rope," shouted Olaf.

The rope was jerked back and fore as the giant fish thrashed in the bay but Angus held on tightly. They got to the shore and tried to pull the Golden Carp onto the beach. It was huge and they could only get it into shallow water. Kirsty ran to Olaf and held the rope as he got out the knife. Olaf waded out and managed to get the knife under a scale near the Golden Carp's tail. He made a cut and pulled out a scale. Olaf ran back to the shore.

"Kirsty. Let go of that rope. I've got another scale," said Olaf.

"Angus let go your rope. We've got a scale," shouted Olaf.

Angus let go of his end of the rope. In a few seconds the Golden Carp untangled itself and swam out into the lake.

Kirsty and Angus laughed.

Olaf grinned, "Well done everyone."

"We better get back," said Kirsty.

They took much less time to get back to the river mouth, as they didn't have to carry the heavy net. Kirsty took one look back at the cavern.

"Loch of the Golden Carp. I wonder if I'll ever come here again?" said Kirsty.

They walked back down the tunnel. In half an hour they had to turn on the glow globe as the luminous algae disappeared. Soon they heard the crashing waves of the sea and arrived back at the cave mouth. The sun was setting and the sea was golden.

"After all that are we too late?" said Kirsty.

"The sun's not set yet," said Olaf. "Come on."

Kirsty and Angus found it much more difficult to climb up the cliff than abseiling down it. Olaf went first and showed them the easiest places to climb. By the time they got to the top the sun was touching the horizon.

"We're too late. We'll never get down to them before the sun sets," said Olaf.

They ran through the Grand Hall and the tunnel to the Hall of Tree Ferns. Lady Morgana was standing in the hall with a group of Sowers.

She gasped and said," You got them?"

Olaf held out the scales.

"While you were away we took Nellbridy and Kerigayle to the courtyard of the Eye Tower. The sun is almost down. Go quickly!"

Olaf ran out of the Hall of Tree Ferns and took a tunnel that twisted upwards. Kirsty and Angus followed. After a few minutes the tunnel opened out to the courtyard of the Eye Tower. Halibutina was standing on the parapet at the top of the tower. Birog and Crok were circling around her. Nellbridy and Kerigayle were lying out on a storm raft of broken tree ferns at the far end of the courtyard. Birog and Crok came flying down to Olaf.

Halibutina shouted down, "Gie thaim the scales!"

Olaf held the golden scales up. Birog and Crok pecked them out of his hands and flew back to the Storm Hags. Birog dropped a scale onto Nellbridy's forehead. Crok dropped the other onto Kerigayle's forehead. The sun set and the sky stars came out.

"We were too late!" said Angus

"Shh!" said Kirsty.

In the moonlight there appeared two glowing golden circles. The circles seemed to melt and spread out over the bodies of the two Storm Hags. Nellbridy and Kerigayle were covered in a thin layer of glowing golden light. Halibutina spun her hands round as she cackled and danced around the balustrade. Suddenly there was a streak of lightning and a crack of thunder. Storm clouds appeared and it started to rain heavily. A wind picked up and circled around the courtyard. Nellbridy, stood up, her tall thin body erect in the storm. Kerigayle got to her feet. Her red hair was flaming around her.

"Wha comes wi us tae fecht Soyean?" shouted Nellbridy.

Angus and Olaf clambered onto the storm raft. Kirsty helped Lady Morgana to get on. Nellbridy and Kerigayle spun their hands in the air and a cyclone formed around the raft. It slowly lifted up into the sky and paused as Halibutina jumped on. A flash of blue fire shattered the top of the Eye Tower as they cleared the Monastery.

The storm raft flew across the Caldera Gardens towards Mount Suil. It was almost like daylight as the lightning flashed every few seconds.

A blue fire came streaking across the sky towards them from the Temple of Suil. The storm raft swerved to the right. Kirsty and Lady Morgana nearly fell off. The raft fell towards Mount Suil. It landed with a great thud in the middle of the Village of the Mind Casters. The Storm Hags got off the raft and headed through the village up the hill. Birog and Crok squawked as they flew overhead. Mind Casters came out of the houses and looked blankly at the procession. Green light throbbed from the scrying stones rotating in front of their vacant faces. One Mind Caster's stone went flying towards Nellbridy. She threw out her hand and a streak of lightning came out and shattered the stone. The Mind Caster fell to the ground.

Another Mind Caster sent flying a scrying stone, and then another. The Storm Hags fired bolts of lightning and destroyed the stones. Each time a stone was hit a Mind Caster fell down.

"Don't hurt them. They don't know what they're doing. They're being controlled by Soyean!" shouted Lady Morgana.

A Mind Caster's stone hit her on the head and she fell down. Kirsty knelt down to see how badly hurt she was. Lady Morgana was unconscious. Olaf and Angus grabbed Lady Morgana's arms and carried her up the hill, behind Kirsty. A scrying stone came flying towards them. Kirsty stared at it and it fell to the ground. They continued their way up the path and came out onto the plateau.

"Ah! Halibutina, Nellbridy and Kerigayle. So nice to see you again!" shouted Soyean.

He was standing on the platform in the middle of the stone circle. Lying against each of the standing stones was a clone of Kirsty. Their eyes were wide open and they all faced towards Soyean. The Brahan stone was spinning in the air above him. Nellbridy threw a thunderbolt at Soyean. It bounced off the air as if the stone circle was enveloped in some kind of invisible force field.

"Temper, temper!" shouted Soyean. He laughed like a demented hyena.

"Now!" shouted Soyean.

Blue beams of light blazed out of each of the clone's eyes and focused on the Brahan stone above Soyean. The stone spun faster and the blue charge built up. A streak of blue fire came flying towards the Storm Hags. They were thrown to the ground, enveloped in some kind of invisible force field. Birog and Crok came flying down and were blasted by Soyean. He turned to look at Kirsty.

"Come to see your sisters Kirsty? Well take a good long look as that's the last thing you will see!" shouted Soyean. "Again!"

Another blast fired from the Brahan stone and hit Kirsty full in the face. Instead of falling over, the light was sucked into Kirsty's eyes.

"More! More!" shouted Soyean.

The blue beams emitting from the clones seemed to grow thicker.

"More!" screeched Soyean.

"Look!" said Olaf.

The clones were changing. Their faces were becoming thinner; their cheeks were becoming gaunt. One of the clones stumbled and the fire went out of her eyes. She crumpled to dust. Another clone fell and the fire went out. Another, then another clone fell until empty cloaks surrounded Soyean. The blue fire stopped pouring into Kirsty and the Brahan stone slowed down its spinning.

Nellbridy, Kerigayle and Halibutina got to their feet. The Brahan stone hovered and then floated across to the Storm Hags and landed at their feet. The Storm Hags held their arms up and made swirling anticlockwise motions in the air. The air spun faster and faster around Soyean creating a vortex.

"No!" screeched Soyean.

He held his arms up as if to ward it off. He was sucked up into the starry sky and carried over the moonlit mountains, towards the Corriekraken Whirlpool away in the distance. Nellbridy, Halibutina and Kerigayle let go their hands. The cyclone instantly died down and Soyean fell into the sea. Everyone watched him by the lightning flashes as he fought against the current. In a few seconds he was swept in a spiral towards the centre of the whirlpool. He reached the centre and was dragged under. There was a rumble of thunder then a crack of lightning.

"Guid riddance," said Halibutina.

"He that blaws in stour fills his ain een," said Kerigayle.

"Ay. Naething like a guid weel tae wash the smot awa," said Nellbridy.

Fareweel

It was a beautiful day and the rays of the sun cast a rainbow across the Bay of Echoes. Olaf the Keeper was standing next to the waterfall on the pebble beach in his new purple robes. The Storm Hags were standing next to him in their best clothes. Nellbridy had on a brand new outfit made from mermaid's purses and kelp. Kerigayle had a trouser suit made from dulse. It matched her red hair. Halibutina wore a dress made from oyster shells and a skullcap of beaded pearls. They all looked very glamorous.

"So Kirsty are you sure that this is what you want to do?" asked Olaf.

Kirsty looked at Angus and asked, "What do you want to do?"

"I want to carry on looking for our parents," said Angus. "They may have been picked up by another boat. If we don't go and look we'll never know."

"I would like to stay and learn more but we must look for our parents," said Kirsty.

"Yese will hae tae come and veesit us," said Nellbridy.

"Yes we will," said Kirsty and gave Nellbridy a hug.

"Ma an aw," said Kerigayle. She gave Kirsty a hug.

"Think on us whiles," said Halibutina. She gave Kirsty and Angus each a hug. Lady Morgana came forward and gave Kirsty a hug.

"I'll always remember you. Safe journey," said Lady Morgana. She sniffed into a hanky.

The life raft had been taken down to the water's edge. Kirsty and Angus walked down the pebble beach with Olaf. Their feet made scrunching noise on the pebbles.

"There's plenty of water in those cartons and the waterproof box is filled with food. I do believe that Halbutina has even put in a pot of her best limpet broth," said Olaf. Kirsty and Angus both laughed.

"Olaf, I'll miss you," said Kirsty. She gave him a hug. His face reddened.

"I'll miss you too," said Olaf.

Kirsty climbed into the life raft. Angus held out his hand to Olaf. He was about to shake it when Angus slapped it.

"Gottcha!" said Angus. He gave Olaf a big hug.

"I'll miss you," said Angus. He climbed into the life raft.

"Maybe one day I will come and visit your world," said Olaf. He pushed the boat off. It floated out into the bay. Angus took up the oars and headed for the gap in the cliffs.

"Fareweel!" shouted the Storm Hags, in unison.

Mind Casters and Sowers were waving from the cliffs as they rowed out of the Bay of Echoes. Kallid was waving, standing next to a herd of goats. The sea was as smooth as glass as they headed out past the cliffs and headed due south. Birog and Crok flew above the life raft for a while then squawked their farewells and returned to the island.

Half an hour later the life raft caught the current that Nellbridy had said they'd find. The life raft moved swiftly towards the east.

"Look," said Angus, "A mist is coming down over the island."

Gruinsoye gradually disappeared.

"Do you think we'll ever find it again?" said Angus.

Kirsty took her scrying stone out of her pocket and held it in her palm. It floated up and began to spin around.

"I can't tell," she said.

The scrying stone fell back into her palm.

The End

120

Glossary of Scots words

Scots	English
aboot	about
ain	own
an	and, if
ance	once
ane	one
anerly	only
aw	also
awa	away
awricht	alright
aye	yes
bawheid	idiot
bemangit	hurt
bide	stay, live
bing	pile
blaws	blows
bluid	blood
bodden	promised
bowie	bucket
brocht	brought
byordinar	unusual
certaint	certain
com	come
cushin	cushion
daes	does
dinnae	do not
doun	down
ee	eye
eediot	idiot
eenou	immediately
daimen	rare
daurk	dark
day-set	sunset
dee	die
deem	doom
fae	from
fareweel	farewell

gae	go
gang	go
gat	got
gaun	going
gie	give
gin	if
gowden	golden
greenin	craving
greet	cry
guid	good
hae	has
happent	happened
haud	hold
haudles	handles
hauf	half
hoised	hoisted
hoose	house
intae	into
ken	know
kent	knew, known
kilt	killed
kin	family
lempet	limpet
leuk ower	look after
lippin-fou	full to the brim
loun	boy
ma	me
mair	more
mak	make
makkit	made
maun	must
mebbe	maybe
mistak	mistake
muckle	plenty, large
murthers	murders
mynd	mind
nae	no
naething	nothing
neist	next
nou	now
o	of
och	oh
oot	out

ootliners	outsiders
ower	too, over
peelie-wallie	pallid, sickly
pou	pull
pouer	power
quean	girl
raips	ropes
richt	right
remeed	remedy
rousle	rustle
saut bree	salt water
shifty	look
shoog	shock
smot	stain, dirt
snuid	fishing line
stairt	start
stane	stone
stap	stop
stealt	stole
stour	dust
strang	strange
tae	to
tak	take
thaim	them
thair	their
thare	there
thareoot	outside
thay	they
thegither	together
think on	think of
thocht	thought
tither	other
twa	two
twa-three	a few
unco	very, uncommon
unner	under
veesions	visions
veesit	visit
veesitors	visitors
wadnae	would not
wairm	warm
wappon	weapon
war	were
watter	water

wee	small
weel	well, whirlpool
wey	way
wha	who
whaur	where
wheeched	whisked
whiles	sometimes
whit	what
whiten	what kind of
whitely	pale
windae	window
wis	was
ye	you
yer	your
yersels	yourselves
yese	you *pl*

Printed in Great Britain
by Amazon

33390988R00069